"You're hurt. I'm going to have a look, but if you so much as touch me..."

He blinked and Kate's hand trembled as she started to push his jacket aside and pull his T-shirt out of his waistband. Under his clothing, he was muscular, taut and seething. She sucked in a breath.

A trail of blood crisscrossed his chest. "You must have taken some buckshot when you were in the trunk." She looked into his face for confirmation.

Again he blinked.

"It looks bad." She still hadn't found the source of the blood trail. Pushing his shirt higher, she brushed his bare skin with her fingertips and he groaned.

A wave of warmth burst inside of her and rushed to her cheeks. She let out a labored breath and stared at the spot just above his heart, marring his perfect chest.

"I'm dialing 911." She stood up, rifling through the stuff on the table for her phone. She reached for it at the same time his hand wrapped around her ankle, pleading for her to stop.

Hot...relentless...inescapable.

Dear Harlequin Intrigue Reader,

Summer's winding down, but Harlequin Intrigue is as hot as ever with six spine-tingling reads for you this month!

* Our new BIG SKY BOUNTY HUNTERS promotion debuts with Amanda Stevens's *Going to Extremes*. In the coming months, look for more titles from Jessica Andersen, Cassie Miles and Julie Miller.

* We have some great miniseries for you. Rita Herron is back with *Mysterious Circumstances*, the latest in her NIGHTHAWK ISLAND series. Mallory Kane's *Seeking Asylum* is the third book in her ULTIMATE AGENTS series. And Sylvie Kurtz has another tale in THE SEEKERS series— *Eye of a Hunter*.

* No month would be complete without a chilling gothic romance. This month's ECLIPSE title is Debra Webb's *Urban Sensation*.

* Jan Hambright, a fabulous new author, makes her debut with *Relentless*. Sparks fly when a feisty repo agent repossesses a BMW with an ex-homicide detective in the trunk!

Don't miss a single book this month and every month!

Sincerely,

Denise O'Sullivan
Senior Editor
Harlequin Intrigue

RELENTLESS
JAN HAMBRIGHT

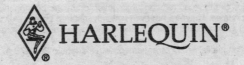

HARLEQUIN®

TORONTO • NEW YORK • LONDON
AMSTERDAM • PARIS • SYDNEY • HAMBURG
STOCKHOLM • ATHENS • TOKYO • MILAN • MADRID
PRAGUE • WARSAW • BUDAPEST • AUCKLAND

ISBN 0-373-88639-X

RELENTLESS

Copyright © 2005 by M. Jan Hambright

This edition published by arrangement with Harlequin Books S.A.

® and TM are trademarks of the publisher. Trademarks indicated with
® are registered in the United States Patent and Trademark Office, the
Canadian Trade Marks Office and in other countries.

www.eHarlequin.com

Printed in U.S.A.

ABOUT THE AUTHOR

Jan Hambright penned her first novel at seventeen, but claims it was pure rubbish. However, it did open the door on her love for storytelling. Born in Idaho, she resides there with her husband, three of their five children, a three-legged watchdog and a spoiled horse named Texas, who always has time to listen to her next story idea while they gallop along.

Jan can be reached at P.O. Box 2537, McCall, Idaho 83638.

CAST OF CHARACTERS

Mick Jacoby—A relentless ex-homicide cop, who now works the auto theft division hunting for a hit-and-run killer, rumored to be a car thief in the Robear family.

Kate Robear—An ex-car thief trying to get her life together and live down her family's reputation by working as a legitimate repo agent, or so she thinks.

Cody Talbot—Kate's four-year-old son.

Otis Whittley—An unfortunate murder victim who knew too much and used the information as blackmail.

David Copeland—Kate's mysterious boss, who's implicated in the Whittley murder.

Dylan Talbot—A man from Kate's past, who holds her responsible for his brother's accident.

Jake Talbot—Dylan's little brother and Cody's father. A man Kate once loved and feels responsible for putting in a wheelchair.

Bret Byer—Mick's ex-partner from Homicide. Unfortunately they were in love with the same woman at one time and he still carries a grudge.

Chapter One

The fat cigar pinched between his gloved fingers glowed orange as he puffed it and stared into the night. The backdrop of the bayou made him feel invisible.

He exhaled his last drag and sucked in a breath of mossy air. The eerie hum of the swamp's carnivorous inhabitants droned in his eardrums. Here in the bayou the cycle of life played out in deadly turnabout. It was his kind of game.

Tearing the soggy end off of the butt, he shoved it into his shirt pocket and flicked the half-finished smoke into the nearby water. It hissed as it extinguished in the brackish muck near the boat he'd pulled ashore. He flexed his hands into fists and felt the leather tighten across his knuckles.

She would be here soon. He'd seen the glow of car lights flicker through the trees on the road to the north. His nerves pulled taut with excitement, anticipation. Like a drug it chased through his body bringing him to arousal.

Beautiful, predictable Kate. He'd chosen well. Caution coiled around his thoughts and constricted his ego. She was a down payment on a bigger prize.

The crush of gravel warned of her approach. He melted into the cocoon of foliage around him, picking up the trail of her movements in the shadows.

KATE ROBEAR COVERED the last ten feet of the road and ducked behind a tree. She leaned against the moss-tangled trunk and peered at the house across the narrow strip of real estate.

A whisper of breeze, heavy with humidity, licked her hair and chased a shiver through her body. Nothing like a late night in a Louisiana bayou to make her skin crawl.

Digging in her backpack, she pulled out her notepad and penlight to study the information her boss had given her on tonight's repo job. Silver BMW 540i, owner of record Otis Whittley. She checked the address scribbled on her pad. It matched the string of black house numbers tacked on the wall next to the front door, where a naked bulb dangled from a couple of bare wires.

The house, if she could call it that, was little more than a shack. Its once-white coat of paint had long ago melted in the Saint Charles Parish humidity, leaving only flakes as a testament. There wasn't anything wonderful about its location, either. Bayou Gauche. The end of the universe.

She released the button on the light, drew in a breath and tried to avoid thinking about what slithered behind her in the stagnant water. She'd never been afraid of the dark, but bayou dark had teeth.

Half-light radiated from the lightbulb and pierced the shadows around the house. Massive oaks dressed in long tresses of Spanish moss swayed in the breeze, mimicking the rhythm of a dancer.

Scanning the dappled landscape, she suppressed her apprehension. She was being paranoid, letting her overactive imagination scare her, but the sooner she got out of here the better she'd feel. Besides, the driveway was empty. She couldn't take what wasn't there.

Frustrated, she shoved her notepad and light into her pocket. Her ride out of this hole was a cell phone call away. Maybe she should abandon her hopes of snagging the car tonight and come back tomorrow.

Kate dismissed the thought and tried to focus. The idea of standing in the swamp all night scrutinizing every shadow wasn't her idea of fun, but hard-to-recover assets were her specialty. There was a five-thousand-dollar bonus for the recovery of the car and she needed it, yesterday.

From somewhere in the bayou the low tone of a car engine hummed to her. Could it be the Beamer? Hope churned her insides. She closed her eyes, listening for the change in the motor's rpms as it slowed for the corners and powered up in the straightaway. It was a BMW. She'd know the sound of its performance 290 horsepower V-8 anywhere and it was coming straight to her.

Adrenaline surged in her veins. She edged around the broad tree trunk as the car's headlights swept her position. She was here for one thing and it was about to stop less than fifty feet away. It was her lucky night.

Her pulse quickened, sweat formed on her palms, it was a rush she'd come to need.

The engine rumbled, then raced as the driver gunned the motor a couple of times and shut off the engine.

She listened for the horn toot of the alarm. Nothing. The lack of a locked door would give her plenty of time to get into the car, start it and drive away.

Otis's footfalls in the gravel were somewhere between a shuffle and a stumble. He garbled the lyrics to "Show Me the Way to Go Home."

The catchy notes of his boozing song amused her. He was drunk. That explained the time. She'd almost feel guilty leaving the poor guy out here in this creepy place with no transportation. Almost.

The creak of ancient wooden stairs and the slap of the screen door were her signal.

She peered out from behind the tree. A single light came on inside the house. Shining through a sheer curtain in what appeared to be a living room. Five minutes and the BMW 540i was as good as gone.

The illuminated hands on her watch pointed to 2:00 a.m. Picking up her backpack from the base of the tree, she dusted the bottom for crawly hitchhikers and slipped it onto her shoulder. The weight of the air had gone two-ton, loaded with rain. There was a storm coming.

As if tapped into her time schedule, the light went out in the front room and came on at the side of the house. The bathroom she guessed. With his pants down, she doubted Otis could beat it out the front door in time to catch her.

She slipped from behind the tree, edging toward the car. Like a soldier on a mission, she focused on the automobile. *Focus, move, attack, drive.* Her method had never failed.

Pausing next to the car, she pulled the dealer's key out of her pants pocket. Repoing a car with the key seemed too easy. She hesitated and looked around, her senses on full alert. The acrid smell of cigar smoke hung in the air. Maybe Otis liked them along with whatever it was he'd had to drink tonight.

She opened the car door.

The shrill scream of the horn blasted.

"Dang!" *An auxiliary alarm?* She jumped in, shoved the key in the ignition and turned it over. The hot engine roared to life. She pulled the gearshift into reverse and tromped on the gas pedal. The headlights came on, the auto locks clicked. The car shot out onto the road in a cloud of dust.

Kate jammed the brake and put the car in drive.

Pop. The screen door splintered against the outside wall of the house.

Her heart jumped in her chest. Otis was loose. Fighting panic, she stomped on the gas. The tires spun, trying to grab the road. "Come on!"

The spinout sent a spray of dirt and gravel out behind her. The tires bit. The car launched forward. She glanced in the rearview mirror as Otis stumbled through the dust.

He raised a long dark object.

Shotgun! Her heart slammed against her ribs. She leaned forward, tucked her head and pushed the accelerator to the floor.

The blast bit through her concentration. Simultaneously, the rear window shattered.

She jerked. Lead tore through metal and raked over her nerves. She straightened and slammed on the brakes. The car fishtailed, she countersteered, stayed on the pedal, feathered the brakes and kept the car on the road.

Cranking the steering wheel hard to the right, she maneuvered the sharp turn at the end of the road and jetted toward the main highway.

A sob formed in her throat, but she reasoned it away. The rear window of the Beamer was gone, but there wasn't a scratch on her.

Should she call the police? Otis Whittley didn't have any right to shoot at her. She was just doing her job.

Kate geared the car down and braked at the stop sign. Highway 306 was in front of her, Otis Whittley was behind her. She took a right and headed for the storage unit she'd rented in Paradise, seven miles away.

The sleek car devoured the distance and she

was relieved when she pulled up next to the storage unit code pad. She punched in the numbers and waited for the wrought-iron gate to open.

If Otis had transportation, she was sure he'd have been right behind her. A couple of people had chased her, but shooting was a first. Other drivers could be outrun, bullets were another story. Maybe she should reconsider her current profession.

A shudder built in her insides, its ripple effect forcing gooseflesh up her arms. It had to be because of the nip of April air that breezed through the missing window. She checked her rearview mirror. The red reflection of her brake lights shone behind her in the darkness, but the trunk lid was higher than it should be. A pellet must have damaged the lock.

The gate swung open and she drove the car to the back of the complex where she'd left a double garage-size unit open. She pulled the car in and killed the engine. The auto locks snapped. She climbed out of the car and flipped on the switch to a single fluorescent overhead.

A shower sounded good. Scrubbing the swamp off her skin was going to be priority one, she decided, checking her watch. Two-thirty a.m. Not bad for a night's work. The paperwork could wait for tomorrow, but she wanted to have a look at the damage caused by the shotgun blast.

Kate rounded the left rear quarter panel.

The notes of a scream raced up her throat, but they came out as a whimper. Caught between reality and disbelief, she watched the buckshot-peppered trunk open without a sound.

"Move and you're dead." A man climbed out of the compartment and rose to six feet of lethal flesh and bone.

Time stopped. She stared at the gun in his hand, then back at his face.

"Who are you?" he asked above the buzz of the fluorescent.

She struggled for words and took a step back, gauging the distance between herself, the man and the open door. Her limbs went numb, the air thickened around her. She worked to breathe, to think. *Stay cool.*

"I could ask you the same thing." She watched his expression for any sign of what was going on in his head. Her backpack was in the passenger seat, but it was too far away for her to reach it before he blew a hole in her.

"Close the door."

She obeyed, taking in his size and weight. How strong was he? Pulling the rope, she brought the metal door down slowly. If she waited until it was almost closed, she could roll underneath it. There was a spare key outside in her Bronco.

"Don't get any ideas." In two steps he was on her. He clamped his hand on her shoulder, but his fingers didn't bite into her flesh. The physical contact jolted her; she froze under his touch. Guys like this got off on the fear they could generate. She wasn't going to give him that satisfaction, or the advantage.

The door touched down on the concrete floor. She had to get to her backpack, somehow.

She turned toward him, determination in her veins.

"Again. Who are you and why did you boost this car?" His voice was low, demanding and cut with an edge of irritation.

"I didn't steal it. I repossessed it." If her answer erased doubt, it didn't register in his sharp green eyes, eyes that seemed to probe into her soul.

"Wouldn't it be better to do it in daylight with a police escort?"

His solution intrigued her, even while the gun he aimed at her made her wonder about his status. Law-abiding citizen or desperate criminal?

"I obtain hard-to-recover assets. Not everyone willingly lets you take their ride."

His expression hardened, his eyes narrowed. "Have you got a lock for the door?"

Fear raked across her nerves. "Maybe."

"Maybe isn't good enough."

This was her chance. Kate took a step back. The padlock was in her backpack. "It's in the front seat. I'll get it." *Move.* She crossed in front of him.

He turned as she passed by and she was aware of him next to her as she opened the door and pulled her backpack out by one strap. She grasped the zipper. If she only opened it partway, she could put her hand in and rummage around. He'd never see his demise coming.

"I'll take that."

Before she could protest, he pulled her lifeline away. She swallowed her disappointment. Was this guy a mind reader?

"Head for the table." He motioned to the card table she used for her paperwork. It was pushed into the corner at the front of the garage. She took hesitant steps toward it. He followed close behind. So close she could feel his heat, feel the arc of his strength connect to her body and drive fear into her soul.

Dressed in black from head to toe. Leather jacket. Early thirties. Clean shaven. Blond. Six-one. Green eyes, yes his eyes were green. She stored the details in her mind for the day the cops caught him. That was, if she lived.

A knot tied her stomach as she thought of her son. She had to make it…for his sake. She stopped at the table, wincing as he slid the zipper on her backpack and dumped it out with a couple of shakes. Her gaze locked on the Taser gun as it fell out with the rest of her worldly goods. An innocent object disguised as a tissue holder.

Attack. She dove for the weapon. Desperation choked her mind and made her movements erratic. She missed her mark and he threw an arm around her waist.

Kate fought to get away, but he was too strong. She ended her struggle, aware of the feel of his hard chest against her back and the sensation of being superheated against him.

"Who are you lady, MacGyver?" He laid his gun on the table, snagged the padlock and carried her to the door.

"I'll warn you once." His breath was warm against her ear, his voice soft, but deadly. He set her down, turned her and pointed his finger in her face an inch from her nose. "If you move, I'll tie you up."

He opened the lock and put it into the clasp on the door.

Kate kept still, watched him snap the lock shut and deposit the key in his left front pants pocket. She had to have the key.

Mick felt better with the lock in place. The woman beside him was trouble and too unpredictable to take his eyes off. He could see her thinking every second. Planning her escape. The challenge sent a surge of excitement through his veins. It didn't bother him that she was the sweetest piece of eye candy he'd seen in an eon, but so far he hadn't been able to get any information out of her that made sense.

The intensity of the burn in his side flared again. He didn't know how long he had until his shrapnel wound sent him to la-la land. If he lost it now, she'd be gone along with the Beamer, his only link to Otis Whittley.

"Where did you get this car?"

Her eyes were a rich shade of coffee-brown and sparkled with defiance. She glared at him and raised her chin.

Mick knew the make-me gesture. He hadn't busted a single punk who hadn't flashed him the same challenge. But she didn't look the part.

Clean Levi's hugged her slim hips and brushed the tops of black running shoes. A black sweatshirt was tied around her narrow waist and a tank top with TULANE printed on it stretched across well-rounded breasts. Shiny hair the color of mahogany was parted on the side and splayed well below her shoulders. He put her height at five-six or so. She looked delicate standing in front of him, but he'd felt the repressed strength in her curvaceous body for himself.

He swallowed and tried to focus his wayward thoughts. "I haven't got all night."

"It's the property of Dallas S & L. I'm supposed to deliver it to them on Friday."

"You don't understand." He stepped toward her, his patience brittle. "This car stays put until you tell me who you are and what you really want with a fifty-thousand-dollar ride."

"I told you. I repossessed it."

"Yeah, and I'm the tooth fairy." He was getting nowhere with her and he didn't have time to mess around.

"Look, lady, I'm not going to shoot you." He raised his hands, feigning peace. "I need information. If you hadn't taken the car, I'd have it." Otis was probably miles away by now.

"Come on." He grabbed her elbow, steered her around the car and back to the table. If she wouldn't tell him who she was, then he'd find out for himself.

He shuffled through the contents of her back-pack, a virtual smorgasbord of paraphernalia fit to rescue a spy from any situation. Rope, a Swiss Army knife, first aid kit, cell phone, even a cache of tissues to blow her perfectly shaped nose. He'd never seen anyone so prepared. But she wasn't going to be prepared for him, if she didn't take him where he needed to go.

His gaze settled on her wallet. He grabbed it, popped the clasp and flipped it open to her driver's licence.

Kate Robear, 415 Murray, New Orleans. Hatred exploded in his chest, burning him like a red-hot poker. He sized up the woman in front of him while the knowledge ricocheted deep into his brain.

He had a Robear? The family resemblance was indisputable. Dark hair, fair skin, expressive eyes socketed innocently in a beautiful face. For an instant he wanted to make her suffer as he'd suffered, but he sucked it up and tossed her wallet onto the table.

Kate studied the slight tic along his jawline, the faraway flicker in his eyes, and waited for the moment she could reach for the Taser.

"Robear. I might have known, no junk for a Robear."

His words knifed into her mind. There was

contempt in his voice. His body stiffened and revulsion flared in his eyes.

What did he know about her family?

As if lost in some distant memory he looked away for a second.

Attack. She grabbed the Taser and jerked to the right, avoiding his bear-paw swipe.

The device came to life like a live-voltage wire. She slammed the weapon to his thigh and pushed the button. A muscle-incapacitating zap hissed into his body. He stumbled back and collapsed.

She fell forward onto her knees and stared at the man laid out in front of her.

His eyes were wide with surprise, but he lay motionless.

She crawled toward him, determined to get the key before the Taser gun's effect wore off. He was fit. It wouldn't take long for him to regain his motor skills. She shoved her hand into his pocket and felt through its contents. Change. Pocketknife. She brushed the elongated metal shaft of the padlock key with her fingertips, pinched it and pulled her hand out.

Sticky red liquid coated her fingers.

Blood.

Her heart raced in her chest as one horrible thought chased another. She stared at the man sprawled on the concrete floor. He was bleeding. Could she leave him here? What if his injury was serious? He could die in front of her.

She slipped the key into her pocket and edged close to him. "You're hurt. I'm going to have a look, but if you so much as touch me, you'll get this again." She jabbed the weapon at him.

He blinked.

Kate's hand trembled as she pushed his jacket aside and pulled his T-shirt out of his waistband. Carefully she moved the blood-soaked fabric up, trying to avoid touching his bare skin. Under all that black, he was muscular, taut and seething. She sucked in a breath. If masculinity was a crime, he'd be doing life, and if he weren't incapacitated, she was certain he'd have her on the ground with his hands around her throat.

The thought of her son slammed into her mind like a tidal wave. She stopped. What would happen to Cody if she wasn't there to take care of him? This man could do that. Take her life.

She swallowed the knowledge and returned to her task. She couldn't let him bleed to death. She had to take a chance.

A trail of blood crisscrossed his chest. "You must have taken some buckshot when you were in the trunk." She looked into his face for confirmation.

He blinked.

"It looks bad." She still hadn't found the source of the blood trail.

Pushing the shirt higher, she brushed his bare skin with her fingertips.

He groaned.

A wave of warmth burst inside of her and rushed to her cheeks. She let out a labored breath and stared at the spot just above his heart and slightly to the left where a pellet had burned a trail, marring his perfect chest.

"I'm dialing 911." She stood up, riffling through the stuff on the table for her phone. She reached for it at the same time his hand wrapped around her ankle.

Hot…relentless…inescapable.

Chapter Two

He jerked hard, pulling her off balance. Her right hand slammed against the tabletop, the Taser dislodged from her grip and clattered onto the floor.

She hit the ground.

In slow motion, he pulled her toward him.

Elbows against the concrete floor, her heart pounded and she kicked, swimming against a wave of fear that threatened to drown her, but he was too strong.

Catching sight of the Taser, she reached for it, straining to touch it in a final desperate move.

One more second and she would be his, but he suddenly let go. Hope for survival surged in her veins. She sat up and fixed her gaze on him.

He pulled himself upright and leaned against the front tire of the Beamer. "Kate Robear. Detective Mick Jacoby. New Orleans Police Department, auto theft division." He held the badge in his hand like a trophy. "Battery on an officer is a crime."

She tried to shut out his words, but an image of Cody staring at her through prison glass was the only thing that came into focus.

"Can't we work this out? You never identified yourself as a cop. I thought you were going to kill me."

He sat very still. His chiseled features as hard as stone. She didn't know if her reasoning could find a catch hold, but she had to try.

"You locked us in here together. I deserve an explanation for that." He continued to watch her with eyes the color of shallow seawater.

"I'm not a car thief." Desperation diced her composure to bits. "This car has been repossessed, legally. I have the paperwork. I didn't steal it."

"Prove it. Take me back to Otis's."

"You can't be serious. You're in no condition to go anywhere but Mercy Hospital."

"I hope you like jail."

Her pulse jackhammered at her temples. He wanted to go back into the swamp?

"You've got a first aid kit."

"You're nuts. He shot at us. At me. Who's to say he won't kill us next time?" The thought rattled her bones.

"Get the kit."

She scrambled to her feet and grabbed the medical supplies she always carried. He had to be crazy if he thought he could do this. Cops thrived on danger, but blood loss didn't take the testosterone level into consideration. He'd be at Mercy before dawn and she'd be in jail or dead. The victim of a drunk wielding a shotgun.

"Put a dressing on it. It'll hold until I get to Otis."

"You need more than a dressing."

He pulled his T-shirt farther up, his jaw locked against the pain. Muscle tensed just under his skin and she watched him stiffen. Desire drummed deep in her body.

"What are you going to do? Arrest him?" She felt his stare as if it was solid, looked into his eyes and pressed the thick pad against his wound.

For an instant he closed heavy-lashed lids over pain-clouded green eyes, but opened them almost immediately.

"Why do I need Otis?"

"How about him shooting at us for starters. And he did this." She nodded to the bandage she pressed to his side. "He assaulted you first."

A half smile arched his mouth, but vanished as quickly as it had appeared. "I have a Robear in custody. I'm doing my job."

She'd taken the family career track? Was that what he thought? "Let's get you to my car before you pass out. You don't have to be conscious when I drive you to the hospital."

He forced his palm down on her hand. Heat burned into her fingers and sent a jolt of current through her body. She tried to pull away, but couldn't escape his touch or the awareness it evoked.

"You will take me to Otis." He was so close, she could see beads of sweat form on his upper lip. "If you don't, you'll serve time when I'm done with you."

"Okay. Okay!"

He released his hand from hers and she felt him shudder.

"I'll open the lock." Kate moved away from him and fished the bloody key out of her pocket. If she didn't get him out of here soon, he'd pass out.

Hand shaking, she fit the key into the padlock and raised the metal door. He was on his feet by the time she returned to his side. He slid his gun into the waistband of his pants. At least someone could shoot back this time.

"Get your stuff, MacGyver." He glared at her. "Nice and slow."

Kate jammed her things into her backpack

and zipped it shut. There was no way out except going into the bayou with him.

"His place is about seven miles from here on the edge of Bayou Gauche." She pulled his arm over her shoulders.

He walked on his own, but leaned heavily on her, pressed close to her side. His body heat radiated into her and pulled her nerves thin, doubling her discomfort, but she couldn't run away. Couldn't escape the myriad of opposing sensations that targeted her mind and body.

A fine drizzle fell outside. She settled him into the passenger seat of her Bronco and hurried around to the driver's side. Kate started the engine and rolled out of the lot, letting the flip-flop of the windshield wipers calm her nerves. What a mess she'd gotten herself in tonight. Life had just become immensely more complicated thanks to the angry, wounded cop in the passenger seat next to her.

"You do know you're in the middle of my investigation?"

She gave him a sideways glance and refocused on the road. "I didn't know cops liked to hide out in car trunks. You're in the middle of my repo job."

"A man's got to get creative. You picked a bad night to take his ride."

"Some ride." Kate killed the lights as she made the turn just short of the house. "No sense getting him fired up." She cut the engine, rolling the last twenty feet. She'd learned to be quiet and invisible. "There it is."

The single bulb over the house numbers still burned in the darkness. The bathroom light shone at the side of the house.

"Just like I left it. He's probably in his crib, sleeping like a baby.

"How did you find this place?"

"My boss gave me the information."

Mick pulled his pistol out of his waistband and checked his rounds. "Who is this boss of yours? Has he got a name?"

"I don't give out that information."

"You will." He snapped the cylinder shut. He'd catch Otis in his bed, arrest him and take him downtown. Any leads he'd have gotten with the tracking device in place were gone now, but he had her. It wouldn't surprise him if she knew more than she was telling.

The pain in his side had turned to a dull ache. He'd been in rougher shape a couple of times, but he'd never been assaulted by a Robear. Certainly not by a female one who was short on details and long on looks. He hadn't even known the strange breed existed, until tonight. "Stay here."

He climbed out of her Bronco and stood still, listening to the sounds of the night. The rain had stopped, but there was a dampness in the air that penetrated through his skin. He turned the collar up on his jacket. It had been a long time since he'd been in the bayou without the sun overhead. He glanced at Whittley's house and scanned the darkness.

The night was strangely still. His caution level rose. Beyond the thick mesh of trees protecting the house, he heard movement in the water. A slow rhythmic slosh, like the dip of a paddle. Then it stopped. Probably an alligator courting a meal.

Striding across the road in a zigzag pattern, he made it to the porch. A rickety stairway approached the front door from the left. He stepped up onto the first stair. The rotten wood moaned under his weight. He skipped the next two and made the landing without a sound.

The screen door dangled from a single hinge. Otis had been in some kind of a hurry to stop Kate from taking the car.

He leaned to the left of the entry and balled his fist. Bang, bang, bang. He pounded the door and listened to the sound echo inside. "Otis Whittley. New Orleans police. Open the door."

No response.

He didn't have a warrant. If Otis didn't come out willingly, there wasn't much he could do.

"He's not here."

The element of surprise was usually his, but he whirled around at the sound of her voice. Kate stood on the step below him. "What the... get back in the car."

"He's not here. I looked in all the windows."

"You did what?"

"I'll show you." She brushed past him, turned the knob and gave the door a push.

It swung wide-open. A shaft of light from the outside bulb penetrated the front room.

She moved to step over the threshold, but he pulled her back. "You can't go in."

"And why not?"

The hairs on his neck bristled. "See the broken lamp, the ransacked kitchen?"

"Yeah."

"Something went on here after you boosted the car."

"I didn't boost the car."

"It's a crime scene."

"We've only been gone half an hour. I don't know how anything can happen in half an hour."

"It's as easy as squeezing the trigger. Click. You're dead." He took Kate's hand, ignoring the burst of electricity that arced up his arm and spread through his body. He'd neglected to point out the pool of blood near the end of the hall. Fresh blood.

He marched her closer to the car. Closer to safety. He put her in the passenger side and moved around to the driver's side, eyeing the darkness. Braced for unseen threats that could come at any time.

What was he thinking, bringing her out here? He should have called a black-and-white to take her in. He climbed in and threw a sideways glance at his unwilling passenger. "I need your cell phone. Mine's DOA. Shrapnel."

"Sure."

He watched her rummage in her bag of tricks and pull out the phone. She handed it to him and smiled. His insides went to mush. She was good. There wasn't any doubt about it, but he didn't trust her.

Mick pressed in Callahan's station number and waited for his friend to pick up. "I've got a crime scene." He rattled off the location of the shack Otis lived in. "There's no body. It'll probably go to Schneider. ETA? Fifteen. I'll be here." He hung up and leaned back into the seat, feeling ragged around the edges.

"Body? What are you talking about?"

"I can't involve you." His own words kicked

him in the gut. She was already involved, but just how, he wasn't sure.

"Tell me everything you know about Otis Whittley and his Beamer."

"I told you all I know. I repossessed the car tonight. I don't know Otis. He's just a name on a list."

He didn't want to believe her. Believe she'd just been in the right place at the wrong time? Things didn't happen by accident. "Who do you work for?"

Pulling a penlight out of her pocket, she opened the glove box, shined the narrow beam of light into the compartment and pulled out an envelope. "I have a court order, that's all you need to know."

Who was she protecting? There wasn't an honest person in the Robear clan. Any one of them could steal a car in under thirty seconds and wave as they drove off. Was she any different?

He set his jaw and locked out a minuscule desire to believe her. A Robear was a Robear. They'd taken all they were ever going to take from him.

"I'll have to haul you downtown. My supervisor has a nasty temper in the interrogation room. You'll spill your guts before the bars on Bourbon Street close."

"Where do you get off threatening me? I'm a law-abiding citizen. That car is in my possession and I intend to shuttle it to Dallas at the end of the week."

"You're in my custody." The air temperature in the car went subzero.

"You'll have to arrest me then, because as soon as your buddies arrive, I'm going home."

If he wanted to keep her, he'd have to arrest her. The charge wouldn't hold her for long. The thought tasted like dirt in his mouth, but he was in no condition to drag her there in cuffs, only to have her bond out in the a.m. "As soon as the crime-scene investigator arrives, you're free to go. You're a material witness. I'm going to need a full statement and elimination prints. One of the hazards of touching the doorknob. Don't leave town."

"I wouldn't dream of it." She sat stiffly in the seat next to him.

"Give me the papers." He pulled them from her hand and opened the envelope. She directed the beam of light onto the document.

Mick studied the paperwork, giving the bank in Dallas authority to reclaim its property by any means necessary. As much as he hated to admit it, she was telling the truth, but he'd check to see if she had a record.

"I'd like a copy of these." He folded the papers and shoved them back into the envelope.

"Can do." She flipped the switch on the flashlight, plunging the interior of the car into darkness.

Mick waited for his eyes to adjust in the weak light from the porch bulb.

"Why do you have it in for me Officer Jacoby?" Her voice was soft and low, matter-of-fact.

His nerves twisted around his hatred. "I have it in for anyone who's broken the law." He'd forced the words out. Did she know how much he wanted her to be guilty? Only her court order was going to protect her tonight. "Looks like you're in luck." The CSI team van made the corner with its lights flashing.

She was out of the car before he could finish his sentence. Mick climbed out from behind the wheel and closed the door. They met in front of the Bronco. "I'll be on your doorstep tomorrow morning. You better be there." He wanted to slap the cuffs on her right now and chain her to the nearest tree, but he hesitated.

"You can plan on it, Officer." He searched her angelic face for a glimmer of deceitfulness, but it was his heart that told him she would be there in the morning, waiting.

The CSI van slowed and stopped, followed by a string of other vehicles.

He waved her off, stepped aside and watched her climb in behind the wheel.

"Jacoby, you responsible for this mess?"

Mick turned around as Callahan climbed out of the van and walked toward him. "You know me. If there's a crime, I'm there."

Callahan slapped his shoulder and smiled. "I like your attitude. Sure you won't come back to homicide? We could use you."

"No. I had all of that I could take."

"I understand. Let's have a look."

Mick took him up the stairs and pointed out the pool of blood at the back of the hallway. "I'd say there's a body somewhere."

Callahan shined the beam of his mag light onto the large red stain. "Good-size volume. I'd have to agree. I'll get the team in here. We'll let you know."

Mick felt his body sag and sat down on the top step. His head throbbed and he tried to fight off the shakes.

"You okay?"

"No." He watched Kate's taillights disappear around the corner. Five years' worth of mental compensation had just been spent in forty-five minutes. Five long years of a search that never ended, a search for the car thief who'd killed his wife and daughter during a boost, and never looked back. The rumor was it had been a Ro-bear behind the wheel that night. Was it her? Was she the one?

"Call me a ride out of here, Callahan. I need a gurney."

"You've got it, buddy."

KATE STEPPED OUT of the shower, coiled her hair in a towel and slipped on her bathrobe. She'd let the water needle her skin for twenty minutes, but she still felt like a zombie. Even a couple hours of REM sleep hadn't been enough to erase last night's confrontation with Mick Ja-coby. Maybe the attraction she'd felt toward him was only imagined.

The buzz of the doorbell, followed by a couple of loud knocks, pushed into her brain. Tip-toeing to the door, she looked through the peephole. The focus of her thoughts stood on her front porch. She jerked back. He was even more sexy in daylight. She'd known he'd come around to talk to her, but 7:00 a.m.?

She took a deep breath, undid the dead bolt and swung the door wide. "Good morning, Of-ficer." Her cheerful attitude didn't bring an iota of change to his solemn features, grayed by lack of sleep and blood loss, she guessed, but he was still the best-looking male she'd seen in too long. His formidable self couldn't change that.

"It could be." He moved past her into the house and stopped in the middle of the living room with his back to her.

Kate closed the door and watched him size up the place. His silence and lack of visual contact annoyed her, but the full-on backside view of Officer Jacoby made her heart beat faster.

"Shall I lift the cushions so you can check for stolen cars?" Scurrying to the couch, she lifted the center cushion. "Nothing here. Maybe I keep them under the rug." She stomped her bare foot a couple of times and pulled in a breath as he turned toward her and leveled a stare on her with eyes she guessed never missed a thing.

"Look, Ms. Robear. I didn't come here to search the place... um, your..."

Heat radiated into her cheeks and she felt her face redden as his all-seeing gaze slid down the front of her robe. Reality along with the feel of air on exposed skin made her draw a sharp breath. She squeezed the gaping lapels together. "I'll throw something on."

She hurried from the room, alarmed by the tingle his stare had provoked. She certainly wasn't a prude, but neither was she ready to provide a peep show for a cop.

Closing her bedroom door, she leaned against it. Why was it he always seemed to be judging her? She had the impression he'd dealt with her car-stealing family. Every cop in New Orleans had. He probably thought all Robears were created alike. Born to boost cars and chop them up for fun and profit.

Well, she took cars legally these days, and if it took every ounce of her persuasive power to convince Officer Jacoby of that, then so be it.

Moving away from the door, she picked out a pair of jean shorts and a plain white blouse and put them on. There was no denying Mick Jacoby was a looker, but he was also a man on a mission—something she'd be wise to never forget. But she had a mission, too. Keeping the Beamer and the five-thousand-dollar bonus that went with it. She composed herself and went back into the living room.

He stood in the same spot where she'd left him. She took a second to appreciate the thigh-hugging black jeans molding the outline of his quadriceps. His maroon T-shirt was pulled tight over washboard abs and bulging biceps hooked to shoulders as broad as the liberties she mentally took with his physique. She'd bet he could tell her how many tiles there were on the ceiling of the local gym.

Looking away, she swallowed and tried to put distance between her thoughts and the situation. *Cop. Cop. Cop.* Drilled in her mind.

"How did you do at the hospital last night?" She tossed the question over her shoulder while she moved into the kitchen and scooped coffee into the filter, filled the reservoir and turned it on.

"A single piece of buckshot. I'll live."

Unsatisfied with his answer, she turned around. "How bad?"

"A fraction lower and you'd have hauled me to Dallas."

Nibbling her lower lip, she studied him. He was tense, as if standing in her living room made him uncomfortable. She couldn't have that. "Why don't we sit down?" She'd be doing herself a favor if she was on her best behavior. "I'll pour us a cup of coffee and we can talk."

She hoped he'd position himself on the sofa and relax a bit, but he pulled out a chair at the dining-room table. All business. Her business.

Mick settled into the wooden ladder-back chair, complete with a blue checked seat cushion. If Kate Robear was a car thief, she had to be the best disguised one he'd met. Her small house had a homey feel to it. From the floral sofa to the pictures on the walls, the place held her sultry warmth. He watched her move about the small kitchen. Notes of the song she hummed tickled his ear, but he couldn't name the tune. Her legs were long and shapely. She carried herself like an athlete. If she weren't on his witness list, she'd be on his gotta-have list. He shook his thoughts. She was a Robear. That was all he needed to know. No quaint gingerbread house and a cup of hot coffee was going to change that. He had to concentrate.

"Can we get on with this statement?"

"Oh, sure." She moved into the dining room and set a cup of coffee in front of him. "Do you take cream and sugar?"

"No." Mick flipped open his notepad, anxious to move his thoughts forward. "Last night, did you notice any other car besides the Beamer?"

"No, but there are lots of pull-ins on Bayou Road. I suppose I could have missed seeing a vehicle, if it was parked in the undergrowth."

Picking up his cup, he took a slow sip, eyeing her over the brim. She looked innocent enough with a towel around her head and large round eyes that crinkled at the corners when she was thinking.

"I had my friend Gabby drop me off. She

waits for me to call her if the mark doesn't show up. Then she'll come out and get me."

"I'll want to talk to her. See if she saw anything."

Mick wrote down the phone number Kate gave him. "What about the man you work for?" She hadn't budged on the point last night. "It'll go a lot better for you, Kate, if you'll tell me who you work for."

"David Copeland. He handles Dallas S & L. I've never had a face-to-face with him."

"How long have you worked for him?"

"A little over six months."

Mick rolled the man's name around in his head. He'd have him checked out. "How does he contact you?"

"He calls me the day before a job. Gives me time to make arrangements for Cody."

"Cody?"

"My son."

Mick's heart rate sped up. She had a child?

"Can you tell me what other cars you've re-poed in the last six months?"

"Sure." She stood up and went to a small desk, opened the drawer and pulled out a notebook. "I keep track for tax reasons." She returned to the table and sat down. "Let's see. October a Porsche 944, owner Stephen Hacker,

1844 Caldwell. In November a Rolls, owner Hugh Keller, 3210 Jasper. I repoed a Mercedes E class in December from Nathan Morris."

Mick jotted down the make of the car, date and name of the owner. "Address?"

"Looks like 4060 Lindstrom, on the west side. Nice neighborhood. In January, it was a Porsche purchased by Jacob Estes, 4028 Garnet. In February, a red Mercedes convertible, owner Thomas Romaro."

Mick's internal alarm went off at a million decibels. Thomas Romaro was the victim of an unsolved homicide. His buddy Schneider was working the case. They'd pulled the guy out of the Mississippi in pieces. "Go on. Have you got an address on Romaro?"

"Westside, near the Garden District…1019. In March it was a Jaguar XJ belonging to Orlando Durant, 4237 Vivian. Last night I went after the BMW."

Looking up from his notes, he paused, watched her lick her lips and focus her attention on him. The movement shot holes in his control and raised his heart rate, but he didn't drop his gaze from her face.

"It's strange. Every one of these deadbeats lived in an upscale neighborhood, but every house looked deserted except for the car in the drive. None of them were in the garage where you'd expect an expensive car to be parked."

He couldn't agree more, but it was the dead man that interested him. Maybe it was just a co-incidence, but maybe not. "I need a date and time you repoed Romaro's Mercedes."

He watched her run a long delicate finger down the list, wondering what it would feel like against his skin and not as a woman administering first aid.

"Looks like February 14. Valentine's Day. I think it was around midnight because I asked my date to bring me home early."

"You don't sound too disappointed." Mick watched her think; her eyes crinkled at the corners as she looked him square in the face.

"You could say we disagreed, but my love life isn't open for questions, is it, Officer?"

He liked the challenge he saw flash across her face, then vanish into the smile on her lips. Why was she being so compliant this morning? Belligerent, he could handle. Maybe she was feeling guilty for sticking it to him with a hot Taser, or was it something else? Perhaps a little charm as lubricant to wiggle out of an uncomfortable situation.

"We'll call it good for now, but don't leave town." He watched her face go placid and knew she was thinking about the Beamer and a road trip to Dallas. "How much do you make recovering assets?"

"More than you make getting shot at."

"Tell me. What do you do with all that cash?" He wanted to push her. Money made people do strange things and she wouldn't be an exception.

"I give to the needy."

"I suppose that's a worthy thing to do." He felt anger charge through him. Hell, he deserved it, probing into her business. It looked more and more like she was for real, but he had to check out the list of marks on his notepad before he let her off the hook completely.

"I need to get your prints. We can do it here, or you can come into the station. What'll it be?" She swallowed and looked straight at him, her expression trepid. The idea of entering the station frightened her? His suspicion bubbled up.

"I'll come in this afternoon."

"Great."

The front door of the house flew open and a little boy burst into the room. Two steps behind him lagged a young woman.

"Mommy." He threw his arms around Kate's neck and knocked the towel loose from its coil. Her hair spilled over her face and he listened to her laugh. Soft, sweet, genuine.

"I missed you."

"I missed you, too. Did you treat Molly good?"

"Yeah."

An awkward ache moved inside him as he watched the exchange, sucked into memories of years past and lives lost.

She smoothed her hair back. "Cody, this is Officer Jacoby. He's a policeman."

"Where's him's uniform?" The little boy looked up at him, determined to discover why he didn't look the part.

"Well, not every policeman wears a uniform. Sometimes they wear plain clothes and look just like you and me. Isn't that right, Officer?"

He stared down at the handsome little boy, with eyes the shade of his mom's. Thoughts of his own daughter churned in his mind and scrambled his words before they could make it onto his tongue. He nodded and found his voice. "That's right. Sometimes we don't want the bad guys to know we're around." He pulled his badge off his shoulder holster and held it out. "Here's my badge."

Cody ran his hand over the shield. "Wow."

The understanding of a child only encompassed a simplicity. He was free to be impressed minus all the muck that went with the job.

"It's nice."

"It's nice when it gets the respect it deserves." He looked into Kate's face and saw a hint of doubt, but he didn't need her respect. He needed the answers she could give him. How close was she to this case? How much did she know about that night five years ago that ripped his world apart? "Here's my card. Call me if you think of anything else." She took it from his fingers and slid it into her pocket.

"I've gotta go." Mick put his badge on and tried to cram his emotions into the mental box they'd escaped from. "I'll expect you at the station."

Chapter Three

Mick stepped out onto Kate's front step with her right behind him. He paused, scanned the street and looked for the source of the cautionary impulses that shot in and out of his brain. "I'm going to check out the names on this list." He turned toward her. "I plan to have the Beamer impounded."

"You can't do that." She touched him. A wave of heat flamed up his arm. "The bonus on that car pays my bills. If you lock it up, I can't collect."

"The law is the law. The owner of record is missing. He was under investigation for his involvement in an auto-theft ring." He looked into her face and waited for a response, some inkling that she understood his decision. But determination had set her jaw.

"How long before I get it back?"

"The lab will dust it for prints and search for physical evidence. We'll need to determine if Otis committed any crimes with the car."

"This is because I'm a Robear, isn't it?"

"No."

"You think because of what my family did for a living, it automatically makes me a car thief, too? Well you're wrong, Mick Jacoby. You're dead wrong and sooner or later you're going to have to stop hating Robears."

She pushed the front door open and slammed it shut in his face.

Mick stood perfectly still on the step letting her words soak through his thick hide. The truth stung like a yellow jacket. Had he become so jaded he couldn't tell the good from the bad anymore? The day was when he'd had more faith in people, but the sun had long since set on that delusion. He shrugged off her observation and took the steps quickly. Once he reached his car, he scanned the street again and tried to shake the unease that gnawed at his mind and set his nerves on edge.

The cars parked in the street were all unoccupied. He watched the wooded area directly across the roadway for movement. Nothing.

If she was being watched, it would have to be by a phantom, because nothing was out of the ordinary. He climbed into his car and fired the engine.

KATE LEANED AGAINST the front door feeling the full effect of Mick Jacoby's heat. He had it in for her, but how deep would he dig?

"Kate, what's going on?" Molly asked.

"Nothing, just a cop with an attitude and an appetite for Robears."

"Well," Molly whispered, "he can take a bite out of me anytime."

"You goof." She had to admit there wasn't much wrong with the Mick Jacoby package—fair hair, light green eyes—a surfer stranded on dry land, with enough muscle distributed in all the right places to make any woman fake drowning. "Okay. He's hot, five million degrees, but cops aren't my style."

"Emm." Molly wagged her finger in Kate's face and moved toward the door. "I'd make an exception for that one."

"No way."

"All the same, you need a man in your life. Someone safe."

"Where have you been, sweetie? Cops are about as safe as a five-year-old with a lighter."

Molly grasped the knob. "Okay, you've got a point, but maybe you won't ditch the idea completely?"

"Maybe." She hugged her friend. "Thanks for taking Cody overnight."

"No problem." Molly waved and strolled down the sidewalk to her SUV. She climbed in and pulled away from the curb.

Kate was about to go back into the house when she noticed the sleek black car on the opposite side of the street, exposed now that Molly's Suburban was gone. Normally it wouldn't have bothered her, but the windows were black. Tinted to the point she couldn't see inside the vehicle. A customized Honda?

Riding a wave of caution, she hurried inside and closed the door. She was being silly, but she'd never seen the car in the neighborhood. She looked around and spotted Cody on the sofa, TV remote in hand and *Rugrats* on the screen.

She plopped down next to him and rubbed his head. "So what did you and Molly do yesterday?"

"Nothing, Mom. Just went to the zoo and saw the animals. I got some candy and we came home."

"That's not nothing, Cody. Did you thank her for taking you?"

"Yeah."

"Good job." She planted a kiss on his dark head and smelled his hair.

"Shall we go to see your daddy today, before you leave?"

"No. It smells funny."

"We make exceptions for people we care about, son. Your daddy needs to see you."

"Okay." Cody fiddled with the remote. "He lets me push him's buttons."

She patted his leg. "That's better. I'll dry my hair and we'll go." She stood up and felt the weight of guilt turn solid in her stomach, as it did every time they went to see Jake Talbot, Cody's father, a twenty-eight-year-old man strapped in a wheelchair for the rest of his life. A man she'd put there with a dare.

MICK SAT NEXT TO Sergeant Schneider's desk with the Romaro file in his hand. "His address of record is Taft Street?"

"Yeah, real dump. I talked to the landlord. Said the guy was four months behind on his rent, claimed he hadn't see him for almost a month. He opened the apartment, and damn if the refrigerator hadn't seen the guy in a month, either. The power had been shut off and the place was a stinking mess."

"Real winner, huh?"

"Yeah."

Mick studied the autopsy photos. "So any idea who diced the guy?"

Schneider shoved a toothpick between the

gap in his front teeth and rocked back in his chair. "Always looked like a revenge kill to me. Up close and personal, but I could never connect the dots. The crime lab didn't find any trace evidence on the body. He was probably killed somewhere else and dumped in the river. No way to know where he went in. The killer didn't try to weight the body, guess he knew Mississippi mud does a scrub job."

"Did you talk to Romaro's family?"

"Nobody to talk to. Couldn't find a thread to unravel. It was almost like the guy appeared out of nowhere."

"An alias?"

"That's my guess, but he had ID on him."

"Prints?"

"We ran him through AFIS. No record."

Mick laid the file on the edge of Schneider's desk, frustrated by the lack of information. The address Kate had given him for the house where she'd repoed the car was nowhere near the victim's apartment.

"I've got a list of deadbeats." He pulled Kate's list out of his notepad. "My witness repoed Romaro's car along with the rest of these guys. Let's run them and see what shakes."

"No problem." Ben took the list, eyeing it carefully. "What do ya know."

"You got something?"

"Orlando Durant. I can't believe he bought a car. Stealing them is more his style. I got a fax a couple of days ago from the Michigan State Police. They caught him doing one hundred forty up I-75, headed for Canada. He was sitting behind the wheel of a brand new Maserati registered in his name. The kicker is there was a suitcase full of money in the trunk. They're holding him for reckless driving and eluding an officer. We've got first claim on him, but he's fighting extradition."

"Let me guess. Grand theft auto."

"Bingo, but there's more. He's claiming someone in Louisiana wants him dead."

"Running scared?"

"Looks that way."

"How soon are we going to get him back?"

"Couple of weeks, if finance coughs up the money."

"I'd like to interrogate him, maybe he knows something about Otis Whittley."

"I'll let you know as soon he arrives."

"Thanks, Ben." Did Kate know Orlando Durant? "I owe you one." He stood up and moved for the door.

"Anytime. Hey, I had a visitor this morning."

"Oh yeah, who?" Mick pulled up short and turned around.

"Byer stopped by for his annual how-the-heck-are-you chat."

Mick thought of the ex-partner who'd saved his butt more than a couple of times, but they'd fallen out of touch over the years. "How's he doing? Staying out of trouble?"

"You know Bret. He's top dog over at customs. Sitting on big money and bigger benefits. Something to do with manifest approvals."

"I heard that, but then he always pushed to get ahead. Not like you and me, happy to be at the bottom of the food chain."

Schneider smiled. "I wish the sharks at the bottom of the food chain would chew my butt off before next week. I've got to pass my physical."

"Good luck." Mick left the homicide division with a smile on his face. He hadn't thought of Bret in at least a year. They'd grown up in the same town in Florida, attended the same college and played on the same football team. They'd become fast friends and eventually went through the academy together.

His cell phone rang. "Jacoby."

"Officer?"

He recognized Kate's voice, laced with panic. "Kate. What's wrong?"

"You better come out to the storage unit. There's been some trouble."

"I'll be right there."

KATE STOOD AT the storage-lot gate, her face the color of a sun-bleached sheet. She put in the gate code and climbed in beside him.

"Did you touch anything?" The question came out like an accusation and he instantly regretted it.

"I'm not an idiot."

"I'm sorry." He touched her hand where it lay on the seat and felt her warmth invade the dark places in his heart. He put his hand back on the steering wheel where it belonged and made the turn down the row of units.

The door to the large unit at the end was open, the butt of the Beamer visible. "It's still there."

"You should see the inside."

He braked and popped the gearshift into park. "I'll get the lab boys over here and deal with the fallout later."

"Fallout?"

"This car should be in impound. I should have called it in last night." He looked at her, caught by the way her mahogany-colored hair framed her face and curled up on the ends. She was a beautiful woman. A flash of desire pulsed through him and settled in his gut.

"I wish it was there, too. I'm probably going to lose my job over this."

"Don't panic. Let's have a look." He got out of the car and moved into the storage unit. Except for the bullet holes in the trunk and the shattered rear window, the car was pristine. He bent closer and looked into the side window. The seats had been slashed and lay open. Stuffing littered the floorboards, white and billowy like a collection of clouds.

"Who else knew about this place."

"Just us. For security, I never told anyone where I took the cars. Not even my boss."

Mick straightened and moved around to the front of the vehicle. Caution slid through his veins and he stopped, but before he could warn her to stay back, she was beside him. He heard her sharp intake of breath.

DIE SLOW KATE. The words were painted across the windshield in dark red.

"Go outside." He leaned close to the glass and drew in a smell of the substance on the windshield. The iron-rich odor turned his stomach.

Blood.

He backed away and pulled the handheld radio off his belt. "Dispatch, officer 557. I need a lab team at A-1 Storage in Paradise, unit B-3." He was guessing, but whoever's blood had been used to paint the message was more than likely dead. His hunch was it belonged to Otis Whittley.

Kate stood outside the unit, her face in her hands. He moved toward her and felt an over- whelming need to protect her from the ugliness inside and the danger outside. "I'm sorry you had to see that." He stepped next to her. "It's probably just an idle threat made by some punk kid."

"Is it…blood?"

"Yeah."

She leaned into him, taking him by surprise. Like a bomb hooked to a physical timer, de- sire exploded inside him and he craved her like air. He put his arms around her and pulled her against his chest, satisfied when she re- laxed into him. "The Beamer will go to evi- dence, then to impound. If the lab confirms it's blood on the windshield, you're looking at posttrial before the car is released." The return of the BMW wasn't his worry. The threat both- ered him.

"Do you think we were followed last night?"

"That would be my guess."

"Maybe not." She looked up at him and he saw a flicker of fear in her eyes.

"What do you mean?" He released her and

stared into her upturned face, watched her swallow, and look away.

"I came over here this afternoon."

"What!"

"I wanted to make sure you hadn't had the car hauled away. It's my livelihood. After you left this morning, there was a black car parked across the street. I couldn't see the driver or get a plate number, but after I went inside, it took off. I thought I was just being paranoid. I took Cody to see his dad, and we made a swing by here."

"We have no idea what's going on." Mick grasped her upper arms. He had to infuse some caution into her.

"It didn't seem important."

"Everything is important. The threat on the window doubles it."

"Look, Mick, I can take care of myself."

"Where is Cody?"

"He's with my friend and her family. They took him to Disney World for a week."

He relaxed his grip on her and dropped his arms to his sides. "Do you have somewhere else you can go besides home?"

"I suppose."

"Go. Chances are whoever did this watched

your house this morning and followed you here. It's not safe. Someone means business."

"I can't leave."

"Look at me."

She complied, staring into his eyes, making his heart race as he searched her face, hoping she didn't fight him. "This isn't a polite request. It's an order. If I didn't think you were in danger I wouldn't ask you to leave. It's better to use caution." He touched her arm and a zap of heat infiltrated his system.

"How long?"

"As long as it takes to get a handle on this case."

"I have to put my life on hold while you look for a handle?"

"It's a lot more interesting to hunt Robears than to try and reason with them." He wanted the words to stick, to raise her awareness level to the danger he could feel in the air, but she gave him a sly smile instead.

"You'll have to hunt me if you drag this out."

"Understood." She smoothed a stray strand of hair and tucked it behind her ear. He didn't doubt she would run if given the chance.

KATE GLANCED in her rearview mirror at Mick's headlights. It was comforting to know he was behind her. A foreboding she couldn't shake had taken hold of her at the storage unit and its grip was unrelenting. Did someone have it in for her? Mick certainly seemed to believe it. Should she believe it, too?

Flipping her blinker, she pulled down the quiet street lined with little square houses. It wasn't the best neighborhood, but it was one she could afford. She parked in the driveway, turned off the engine and climbed out of the Bronco.

Anxiety bubbled inside of her. The early twilight air held a trace of humidity, but it wasn't cold. Somewhere nearby a dog barked, probably at the end of a chain or shut up behind a backyard fence. The smell of a barbecue hung in the air. All was well. There was no visible cause for her feelings.

Mick pulled into the driveway and got out of his car. She studied him in the glow of the porch light as he moved toward her, like the hero in a vivid dream. Maybe he was the source of her unsettled emotions.

"If you grab a bag, I'll take you to your friend's house. I want to make sure you're not followed."

"You don't have to coddle me." She took the steps slowly. "I'm not helpless."

"I'm painfully aware of that, but you are the

focus of my investigation and it got personal today." He was right behind her.

Turning on him, she prepared to reason herself into her own bed, but his features were hardened with determination.

"Don't even, Kate. Never mind that you can take care of yourself. I need to get some sleep tonight and if that means you stay somewhere safe, then so be it. Would you rather I slept on your couch?"

A twinkle of mischief sparkled in his green eyes and she tensed as anticipation hatched in her mind and flowed into her bloodstream. "I'll get my bag." A night with Officer Jacoby a short distance away was more than she wanted to deal with right now.

She pushed her key into the lock. The door gave against the pressure and creaked open.

"Mick…" Terror sizzled through her veins.

"What is it? What's wrong?"

"The door's been jimmied." The sound of gunmetal against leather alarmed her, as he slid his pistol from its holster.

Was someone inside? Waiting?

Mick reached for Kate and pulled her behind him, taking her place on the step above. He stayed to the left and pushed the door all the way open.

In the back of the house he saw movement. For a brief second a human silhouette appeared in the hall and disappeared into another room.

"New Orleans police. Come out with your hands up." He reached inside and flipped the living-room light on.

The once-cozy place was trashed. The sofa and chairs had been sliced to ribbons. Pictures lay on the floor with the glass smashed out. Chaos reigned.

"Go to my car." The house was as still as death, but he'd seen the room the suspect was hiding in. "Lock the doors and stay down."

"Okay." She shuffled off the steps behind him and a measure of relief invaded his body. The perpetrator would have to go through him first.

"Come out. No one has to get hurt." Mick crept into the entryway and scanned the dining room and kitchen. All clear.

Footsteps echoed on the other side of the kitchen wall, then the distinct snap of a window latch clicked.

He hugged the wall. Gun ready. His heart pounded in his ears as he slipped down the corridor and paused outside the room. "This is your last chance. Give it up." The sound of the window being opened reached his ears. In an instant the suspect would be gone. Movement at the front door caught his eye and his heart slammed into his ribs.

Kate stood in the doorway, her eyes filled with terror.

A knife, inches from her throat.

Chapter Four

A split-second decision solidified. He darted into
the dark room, grabbed the man who was halfway
out the window and locked him in a choke hold.

"I don't have anything, man."

Mick patted him down and shoved him toward the doorway with his gun aimed at his
temple. "Why are you here?"

"Let me go. You can't do this."

"Wanna bet." He squeezed until he heard his
prisoner gasp for air. "What are you after?"

Pushing him into the hall, he sucked in a
breath and froze in place.

The suspect had a counterpart, and he had Kate.

His brain fired in rapid succession as he formed
a plan. He forced the thug into the livingroom.

"Looks like a standoff." Focused on Kate, he
willed her to be calm. "How about a trade? You
let her go, and I'll turn over your friend."

A navy-blue ski mask covered the man's face, but Mick pulled in every available detail about him. The man's hand trembled; his breath was labored with excitement. He lacked the smoothness of a career criminal. That fact alone made him more dangerous. Mick tensed and moved closer.

"We'll swap and you can disappear, but if you hurt her I'll put a bullet through your head."

The assailant looked around, wide-eyed. "Let's do it."

Mick moved him to the front door, careful to leave enough room for them to escape. "On three."

He nodded his head.

"One…two…three." Mick released the punk at the same time the assailant let go of Kate. He lunged for her as the two masked men bolted out the door.

In one swoop he wrapped his arms around her and pulled her away from the doorway. His pulse thundered in his ears and he held her next to him. Outside a car engine fired. Tires squealed on pavement and the men vanished into the night.

"Are you okay?"

"Yeah. I'm pretty stirred up, but I'm alive."

She was alive, nestled against him. He pulled

in a breath and caught the whisper-sweet scent of her hair.

"That was risky."

He held her back and stared into her upturned face. Kissing her came to mind, but he reined in the thought. "There's always a risk where a hostage is concerned. I wagered he wanted his accomplice more than he wanted you or a bullet in his head."

She reached up and cupped his cheek with her hand. The gesture sent sparks through him.

Stepping back, he pulled her hand away. "Just doing my job." He'd come too close to kissing her. Too close to crossing the line. "I'll check the bedrooms and call in forensics." He stepped away, moved down the hall and swept the rooms before returning to the living room, where Kate had positioned herself on the remains of an upholstered chair.

"It's all clear."

"Would you look at what they did?" She let out a small moan and scooped up a picture of herself and Cody, setting it carefully back on the shelf where it belonged. "I'd offer you the couch, if I had one."

"Don't touch anything." Mick eyed what was left—a pile of fabric and stuffing. "You're coming with me. This is no coincidence. The MO looks identical to the job on the Beamer. They could come back. I'll take you somewhere safe."

"This scares me. What if Cody had been here with a sitter?"

He watched her very own words force the color from her face. She stood up.

"Don't get riled up, Kate. They were looking for something. We just have to figure out what."

She paced back and forth in the small room, making him nervous. "I don't have anything. No jewelry." She looked around the room. "My stereo equipment is still here."

"Don't try to guess what motivated them. Did you see anything that could help?"

"They were driving the black car I saw this morning."

MICK STOOD IN THE HALLWAY. The first rays of dawn were pushing between the slats of the blinds, reminding him morning was here. The moment stalled in time as he watched Kate, asleep on his sofa.

Every safe house in New Orleans had been full last night, so he'd brought her home. He smoothed his hands over his head. He'd offered her the bed, but she'd refused. Why did she have to look so damn beautiful, snuggled against the white pillowcase, her mass of dark hair tousled around her face? Beautiful, yes. But innocent?

He ground his teeth together. He didn't trust Kate Robear with his mind, but his heart had other plans. How could he separate the two? Had his years with the New Orleans PD made him into the man he was or just kept him alive while he hunted for answers?

Turning around, he went into the bedroom and closed the door. He'd let a Robear spend the night in his home. A home that had sheltered his wife and daughter before they'd been killed. Four walls that still echoed with sounds of their lives. For all of Kate's claims of innocence, her blood ran with Robear genes. She couldn't be trusted. Maybe it was a good thing she was here so he could keep an eye on her.

Mick cranked on the sink faucet in the master bathroom and soaked a washcloth in hot water. He couldn't let Kate get under his skin. It was easier to mistrust her than to give her credence. He pressed the cloth to his face and warred with his choices. Could he pass up the case and risk never knowing who killed his family? Could he let her walk and kiss his only chance at the truth goodbye?

Anger churned his insides. Indecision wasn't

his thing. There was only black and white. Gray had never colored his decisions…until now. He couldn't let her go.

KATE AWOKE WITH A START. Where was she? Looking around the room she settled back against the sofa cushions as last night's memories surfaced. She was on Officer Jacoby's couch. She sat up. A mess waited for her at home. She had to move, had to focus.

Shuffling into the kitchen, she spied the coffeemaker. His home was neat and tidy, not the typical bachelor pad she decided, as she opened the cupboard above the pot. Sure enough, a plastic container of coffee sat amongst perfectly positioned boxes of Earl Grey, English Breakfast and green tea. Sexy *and* organized.

She pulled the canister down and filled the coffee filter, then filled the reservoir at the sink. Flipping the switch to brew, she returned to the couch and folded the blankets.

A fireplace dominated the end of the room and she drifted to the mantel, adorned with photographs in various styles of frames. It looked more like a shrine than a casual grouping.

Every picture contained a woman and a little girl. Each one seemed to catalog a stage in the child's life. The woman smiling back looked happy.

Her gaze settled on a picture in the middle. Mick held the little girl on his knee and the woman stood behind him with her hand on his shoulder. She felt like a snoop, digging into caches where he kept his private things. The woman's wedding ring was obvious. She looked at Mick's left hand in the photo. The gold of his wedding band gleamed back.

Maybe they were divorced? It wouldn't be something to come up in conversation. She moved past the pictures until she reached the end of the mantel. The last picture was in a sterling silver frame. A date was inscribed. Never Forgotten 5-10-2000.

Odd, a divorce would produce such a feel of finality. She focused on a small object next to the picture frame. Curious, she reached for it.

"Don't!"

Kate froze in midtask and let her arm fall to her side. She turned around.

Mick stood behind her, anger etched in the line of his lips, and a hard stare fixed on her with green eyes that had darkened to the color of jade.

A tentacle of fear wrapped her spine, and she swallowed. "I'm sorry, I was just wondering what it—"

"It's mine. That's all."

His short answer stirred her curiosity, but she'd respect his privacy. If he wanted to leave a small chunk of metal on his mantel, who was she to question his reasons?

"I want to go home."

"You can't go home." He moved toward her and stopped. "Not until we catch the guys who slashed things up."

"That could take weeks, maybe months. I have a life."

"No, you don't. Not until we get them."

She stared at his bare back as he strutted into the kitchen, the defensive set of his naked shoulders, the narrow taper of his waist as it disappeared into the waistband of his pants. Liquid desire flowed through her veins unchecked and opened the pores in her cheeks, leaving her hot and embarrassed.

"Coffee?" he asked over his shoulder.

She followed him and watched him pour her a cup.

"Have you considered that whoever is doing this may try to hurt you when they can't find what they're looking for?"

"I'd be an idiot if I hadn't." She was suddenly irritated that he could even think she wouldn't have that horrible thought nested in the back of her mind.

He set a cup on the counter in front of her. "On the surface this looks like burglary or vandalism, but thugs like that rarely make it personal. They don't scribble threats in blood."

She watched him over the rim of the mug as she took a sip.

His jaw tightened and he wouldn't look at her. "I didn't want to alarm you the other night at Whittley's place, but there was blood at the scene. We found marks on the riverbank that indicate a boat of some kind was pulled ashore. There was a cigar butt in the water. The lab is trying to obtain DNA, but the water may have corrupted the evidence."

"Cigar butt?"

"Yeah."

"I smelled it the night I repoed Otis's car." She downplayed the shudder that wiggled up her spine as she mentally connected the information. "They were there, in the bayou…waiting for Otis, watching me? They did the BMW and trashed my house last night?" She willed her frayed nerves smooth. "What now?"

He looked at her. "You hang at a safe house until I apprehend them."

"No way." She set her coffee cup down with

a thud. "If you think I'm going to kick back and let these maniacs keep coming around to screw up my life then you're nuts. I plan to be involved all the way."

"Kate." His tone was soft, like a parent scolding a naughty child. "You know I can't allow you to get involved."

"Not involved? I'm in this up to my neck. If I'm going down, I at least want to know who's pulled me under. I'm not some helpless woman. I can take care of myself."

A nerve played along his jaw as her sharp words cut a path through his macho mentality. She wouldn't let him leave her out. She had too much to lose.

"If you don't let me help, I'll go out on my own. I have all the information I need."

He stepped next to her; inches separated them. She could smell the tang of aftershave warmed by his body heat. She watched the rise and fall of his bare chest, half obscured by a large white bandage plastered on his side. Arousal sparked the nerve endings beneath her skin. He was too close. She stepped back.

Mick couldn't believe his ears. What if she got her pretty little neck…

"I can arrest you, right now."

"What's the charge?" She looked up at him

and smiled. There was something seductive in the line of her lips, something primal. Her feminine charm laced around him and choked off rational thought for an instant. Could he keep her safe, keep his distance, and use her to solve the case? "Obstructing an ongoing investigation. So if I decide you're going to a safe house, it'll happen. You saw the damage they did." He cleared his throat. "It could have been you…or Cody." He hated to scare her, but she had to know.

She nodded.

He felt like a rat playing on her motherly instincts to get his point across.

"I'll do anything you say. I promise." Her dark brown eyes went soft and watery.

Mick reeled his heart in. "We'll start on your list of repos for the last six months. I'm not sure what we'll find, but I hope it's a pattern. By the way—" he looked down at her "—one of the guys on your repo list is already dead. Thomas Romaro. We fished him out of the Mississippi two weeks after you repoed the car. He was killed by a suspect with a penchant for knives."

"Oh no." The color drained from her face.

Mick stepped next to her, took her elbow and guided her onto a stool at the bar. "This is serious. I won't lie to you. We don't know how far these guys will go to get what they want. I got a call last night from Callahan. The lab matched the blood in Otis's house to the blood on the windshield of the Beamer."

"LAST ONE." Mick spun the black plastic trash bag and twisted the tie into place. He stared down at her, focused on the small beads of sweat pearled on her forehead. Her hair was piled on top of her head and pinned into place.

He looked away, cautious of the need that sizzled and cooled inside of him, dragging his mind over a professional line he'd sworn never to cross. She was just another pretty face.

"I'll take it out." He looked around the living room, now bare to the walls. The intruders hadn't left much untouched, but things were shaping up in here much better than in the persuasive department. He'd managed to keep her away from home for a week, but she'd finally talked him into bringing her back to pick up Cody.

"He'll be here in a little bit. I'm going to take a shower, get cleaned up."

"No problem." He watched her stand and brush her forehead with the back of her hand. Her mood had been dark all morning. Mick shrugged his shoulders and headed for the back door. He'd never seen Kate without her spunk. He liked her better talking like a conartist— dodging, twisting and evoking every emotion he'd ever vowed to suppress.

He stepped into the alley and tossed the bag onto the top of the pile. Strangling the thugs who'd done this crossed his mind, but saving Kate that night had been more important than chasing them down. He glanced up and down the alley and reentered the house.

The sound of running water trickled from the bathroom along with a vocal rendition of "Raindrops Keep Falling On My Head." Going into the kitchen, he ran a glass of water and leaned against the counter to soak in the sound of her voice—low, sweet, in tune and sexy as hell.

Dumping the glass, he straightened and looked around the kitchen. It was the only room the suspects hadn't trashed. His gaze settled on the wooden knife block next to the cutting board. The top slot on the right was empty. Mick set his cup in the sink and opened the dishwasher. Empty. He pulled out one drawer after another. Nothing.

"Have you got a search warrant?" She rounded the corner of the kitchen as he closed the last drawer. "The only thing that'll fit in there are toy cars."

"Where's your knife?" He pointed at the butcher block.

"Gone."

"Gone when?"

She pulled out a chair and sat down. "I don't know, a couple of months ago." She worked her fingers through her wet hair. "I think I might have thrown it out in a pan of potato peelings."

Mick felt his muscles loosen up. "Anything else missing that didn't make the police report?"

Crimson crept up Kate's neck and smudged her cheeks. "I just noticed some personal items are gone."

"What?"

"A couple pair of panties."

A sense of concern rubbed around in his stomach. He'd never considered the assailants' motivations might carry a sexual connotation.

"Show me." He followed her down the hall and into her bedroom, careful to keep his eyes on her rather than the king-size bed that dominated the room.

"I keep my things in the top two drawers." She pulled out a drawer and began to rummage through it. She stopped and stepped back. "Oh man."

"What is it?"

She pointed at the drawer. Mick moved in

and carefully picked up a pair of lavender panties. The crotch had been cut out. He dropped
them and picked up another pair with the same
jagged slice pattern. "Sick bastards." He closed
the drawer. "Anything else?" Changing the sub-
ject seemed to refocus her.

"A bottle of perfume is gone from the bathroom."

Worry needled his insides. It was cop worry.
He'd never hunted a sexual predator before he
raped or killed; he'd only come in afterward to
investigate the carnage. Damn, he didn't miss
homicide.

"I'll get this stuff into the report." He turned
and left the room.

"Is that it? Is that all you can do?"

He heard the sound of her bare feet against
the hardwood floor as she paced along behind
him. He stopped and turned around. Her stance
was defensive, her arms crossed in front of her
chest. He waved off the desire to touch her.

"This whole case is expanding like a mush-
room cloud. Crotchless underwear is sexy if you
bought it at a pleasure shop, but not when it's
been tailored with a knife. So far all we have are
attempts, but escalation is the norm and our boys
are picking up speed. They'll keep coming. I'm
going to put you and Cody in protective custody."

"Let's get something clear. By protective, you mean on the run?"

"Yeah."

"How do I tell Cody his life is going to be turned upside down? I won't do that to my son."

Mick saw challenge glitter in her brown eyes. "How do I tell him his mother's dead because she wouldn't cooperate?" He met her gaze and watched her defensiveness soften like ice cream in July.

"You've made your point. I'll pack." He hated to see her defeated, but he let her go, watching her move down the hallway to her room. He hung his head. He wanted the Robears, but not like this. He'd always considered them suspects, never victims. He couldn't get his head around it. The world he knew was on end and so was he.

Striding to the front door, he let himself out onto the front step. The midmorning air hadn't yet reached a high temperature, but it already felt oppressive, crushing, stagnant.

He undid the top button on his shirt and scanned the street, picking up every detail he saw. Brain work, that's what he needed. Something to congeal his thoughts so he could make sense of them. All he had to do was connect repossession, murder, grand theft auto, stalking, vandalism and a missing person. Piece of cake, but where did Kate blend in the mix?

Plopping down on the top step, he worked different scenarios in his mind, but nothing made sense. What was he missing?

A white station wagon pulled up in front of Kate's house and all four doors opened. A group of children spilled out of the late-model car and raced up the sidewalk toward him. Cody was in the lead, a bulky backpack on his back and a fuzzy red teddy bear under one arm.

"Him's a police…man. My mom said."

Cody pulled up at the bottom of the stairs, while two boys and a little girl crowded around him. "Show them your badge."

Mick smiled at the woman coming up the walk behind the kids. She looked frazzled.

"Sure." He pulled the shield off his pants pocket and handed it to Cody. Chaos ensued as each child tried to get a chance to hold the trinket.

"You must be Officer Jacoby." The woman held out her hand. "I'm Linda, Kate's friend."

Mick stood up and shook her hand. "Pleased to meet you. Kate said you were taking Cody on your trip. I've got to admire anyone who can handle children in large numbers."

She smiled. "I need a nap, but everyone had a great time. Where's Kate?"

"Inside."

"Tell her I'll call her after I get these guys home and settled. Too much in-flight soda."

"Sure."

"Okay, load up. If you aren't in the car by the time I count to three, you're toast."

The kids sprinted for the car and he smiled down at Cody, who still held his badge. "Buds, man. That's awesome."

"Yeah."

Mick put his hand on the boy's shoulder. "Things are different since you left."

Cody shifted back and forth.

"Someone messed up your house, but I don't want you to worry because I'm going to find out who did it."

He handed Mick his badge. "Are you going to put your hand cups on them?"

"You bet." He brushed Cody's dark hair and stood up.

Cody bolted up the steps in front of him and ran into the house. Mick followed him in.

He came to an abrupt stop and looked around the empty living room. "I'm getting my scooter," he whispered up at Mick.

Mick shook his head back and forth in warning. "I don't think your mom would appreciate that."

"You're right."

He looked up to see Kate in the hallway, her arms crossed in front of her. "I think the Rollerblade skates are a much better choice. Besides, how often do you get to roller-skate in the living room?"

"Mommy."

"Hey, babe." Kate scooped Cody up in her arms and held him against her. She'd never missed him like this before. Never thought much about their mortality, but the suspect's invasion of their home and life had already left an impression.

"How was Disney World?"

"Good. Emily got sick on a ride. She barfed."

"Yucky."

"That's what Linda said. It got on her shoe."

She hugged him again and set him down. "What's this?" She picked up the fuzzy red teddy bear Cody had dropped at her feet. "Did you win it?"

"No. Him's gave it to me."

Kate looked at Mick.

"Not me."

"Not him's, Mom. The man at the airport."

A chill pierced her and drew fear through her

body like thread at the end of a needle. "What man, Cody?"

"I don't know him's name. At the airport."

She raced to the phone and dialed Linda's cell number. Her heart pounded in her ears as Linda picked up. "Linda, where did Cody get this red bear?"

She paused, listening to Linda explain. "Really? You're sure?"

She hung up the phone and flashed a look at Mick. "She said he had it when they got on the plane for Florida. She assumed he'd brought it from home in his backpack, but I've never seen it before."

Kate sat down in a kitchen chair. Mick stepped forward and took the bear from her hands. He winked at her, sat down and pulled Cody onto his knee. "What did the man say to you, Cody?"

"Him's said, Kate was my mommy. She would like this bear, but I could play with it until I got home."

"Where was Linda?"

"She was there."

"Do you think she saw him?"

"I don't know."

"Did you see his face?"

"No. Him's was behind me."

"Okay." Mick looked over Cody at her and shook his head.

"All right, kiddo, it's time to get your backpack unloaded and put your dirties in the laundry. Socks right side out."

"Okay, Mom." Cody bailed off Mick's lap and raced for his room.

Kate watched Mick's grip on the teddy bear tighten and her pulse jumped. "Am I making too much of this?"

He looked down at the bear and turned it over several times. Every tumble matched the sensation in the pit of her stomach.

"He knew your name. Knew Cody was your son. Knew where he would be that day."

Letting out a labored breath, she tried to pull it together. Reality clawed her mind and sent a mix of fear and resolve into her system. She wanted to grab the bear and tear it to pieces.

The sound of shredding fabric made her jump as Mick jerked the bear's head off. There was something violent about the way he'd dismembered the stuffed animal, as if her thought from a moment ago had somehow landed in his head.

"Would you look at that."

She leaned forward and looked into the small void that had been made in the bear's stuffing.

A coil of paper was pushed into the bear's neck. "Get me a pair of tweezers."

Kate hurried to the bathroom and came out with them, handed them to Mick and got a plastic bag out of the drawer.

He pulled the paper out and laid it on the table. Holding one corner with his nail, he unrolled it with the tweezers.

ANYTIME KATE.

She covered her mouth with her hand to suppress her desire to scream. Anytime he could kill her, kill Cody?

Mick stood up and she leaned against him, glad when he wrapped his arms around her. He was solid, safe, but whoever was doing this knew what buttons to push.

"I'll get this downtown. Maybe they can find some evidence on it."

"It's been to Disney World. Hotels, airplanes, it's hopeless."

"It still goes." He pulled her chin up and she saw determination in his eyes. "We could get lucky."

"I could use some luck right now."

She pulled away and moved toward Cody's room, a plan forming in her mind. She would approach her family. They were the only ones who could protect him, keep him safe until they caught the suspect, or suspects. But how, after all this time? Maybe she should go straight to her father. Kate dismissed the idea. There wasn't much he could do from prison.

What about her brothers? They were scattered, but Frank was still around, maybe he could help. There was Dylan Talbot. Apprehension flooded through her. Could she talk to Jake's brother again? He lived and worked in a subculture she'd managed to escape. Going back wasn't going to be easy.

She poked her head into Cody's room. He was on the floor driving a police car around in a circle. "Hey, you, mind if we talk?"

He shook his head. "Want to drive my fire truck?"

"Sure." Kate sat down on the floor and crossed her legs.

Cody handed her the truck and started to push the car in a circle.

"You probably noticed some guys wrecked our house."

"Mick told me."

"Well, Mick doesn't think it's a safe place for us to be and neither do I."

Cody stopped playing and looked up at her.

"I've decided that you and I have to be apart for a while."

Confusion crossed his baby face and she redirected her message. "How would you like to stay with your grandma Robear?"

A spark of interest lit his eyes. "My grandma?"

"She's a very nice woman. She would take good care of you." Kate warmed to the idea, but it was the state-of-the-art security system around Oak Wood that cemented it. "I want you to pack some fresh clothes in your backpack."

What about Mick Jacoby? Selling the plan to him was going to be like interesting the devil in a shovelful of hot coals. She'd have to work up to it, but it was her decision, not his.

"Okay, Mom." He got up, dropped the car and pulled open his dresser drawer.

Kate stifled the ache around her heart. She planned to declare war on the creeps making her life miserable. She couldn't let Cody get caught in the middle, but what about Mick? Would he put his life on the line for them? Save a Robear? She'd seen the depth of hatred in his eyes. She just couldn't risk her son's life if the answer was no.

WHAT THE HELL was taking so long? He peered into the rifle scope and set the crosshair on

Kate's front door. He flexed his trigger finger a couple of times inside the leather glove. They had to have found the note by now. Kate would send the brat packing via teddy bear surprise. He wouldn't do another kid.

Impatience crept through him and worked him into a sweat. The game was just beginning; he'd paired them well. He pulled a hankie out of his front pocket and wiped his forehead. He was so close to success he could almost taste it, heavy and dark in the back of his throat.

Any minute now they would come outside.

He adjusted his shooting stand and looked into the scope again.

Mick Jacoby filled the lens. He focused on his face and felt his muscles tense as Mick looked straight in his direction. Dead calm slithered through his veins and relaxed his mind. "Bang," he mouthed the word and warmed in anticipation.

Moving the gun a fraction, he spotted Kate behind Mick. Manipulation was a powerful thing. He could make people do whatever he wanted them to. Now to seal it. He released the safety on the rifle, placed his finger on the trigger and sucked in a breath.

Chapter Five

Kate stood in the doorway behind Mick, but he blocked her exit with his body, an impenetrable force she couldn't get around.

"Take Cody. Go in the house." The tension in his voice was solid, it demanded compliance.

"Okay." She fought the urge to run inside and lock the door. What was wrong? What had put Mick in battle stance? She'd have to trust him.

"Come on, Cody. I picked up some strawberry ice cream at the store."

"Can I have two scoops?"

"Three, if you want." She took his hand and hurried him inside.

Mick backed through the door right behind her. He closed it, quickly. "Go into the back bedroom."

She obeyed, fueled by his body language and cautionary tone.

The sound of wood splintering reached her ears.

"Get down!" Mick pulled them to the ground and sheltered them with his body.

Fear shot through her. She pulled Cody close as another bullet tore through the front door.

Silently she prayed Mick would be okay. No macho-cop crap. She could hear him on his radio, feel the whisper of his labored breath against her hair.

"Dispatch, officer 557, shots fired, 415 Murray. I'm pinned down inside the house with two occupants. Fire is coming from a wooded area across the street. Approach with caution."

The radio crackled in his hand. "Copy 557, will dispatch officers to the scene."

Another bullet sawed through the top of the door. Kate hugged Cody tighter, closed her eyes and waited for the nightmare to end.

"Jacoby, you in there? It's clear."

"Yeah." Mick reluctantly let go of her. "Kate?" He touched her back with his hand.

She rolled toward him and opened her eyes. "We're okay."

"Thank God." He reached out and brushed her cheek with his hand. He wanted to tell her he could keep her safe, but he couldn't promise her the sniper who'd just taken shots at them wouldn't do it again.

"What just happened?" She sat up, still holding her son as if she'd never let go of him. He didn't blame her.

"I don't know." Mick sat back against the wall and rubbed his eyes. "I caught a glimpse of something in the woods. It was probably the sun on his scope. He had the power to kill us."

"Why didn't he?"

"I don't know."

A uniformed officer stepped though the front door, his gun drawn. "I've got an officer searching the woods across the street, but the shooter's gone. Do we need EMS?"

"No. Everyone's fine." He helped Kate and Cody to their feet. "Physically, anyway. You okay, buddy?"

The child's big brown eyes were wide with confusion, but he finally grinned and shook his head. "Yeah."

Kate picked him up and leaned against the doorway; her eyes brimmed with tears. She blinked them away and stared at him. "I'm going to take Cody home."

He couldn't believe his ears. He wanted to shake some sense into her. Maybe he'd make her put her finger into one of the bullet holes in her door, just to make it real. "Kate. You can't stay here."

"I know. That's why we're going somewhere where they can't find us. They won't be able to sneak up on us, either."

"And where's that?"

"Home."

Realization needled his heart. She was going home? Back into a world where lawlessness ruled the day. He pulled in his concern and disappointment. She was a Robear. Hadn't he always known that? Hadn't he always been aware of her past?

He looked at Cody snuggled in his mother's arms and mercy altered his judgement. He had to let her make the decisions about her child. He couldn't hold them. Hell, he hadn't been able to protect his own family.

"How soon do you want to leave?"

"Tonight."

KATE SAT ON MICK'S SOFA watching the flames in the fireplace. She'd closed the blinds in the room to shut out the gathering darkness. Every passing minute seemed to tick by slowly in her head. She was going to see her family again. Turn over her most cherished gift to them for safekeeping, but it was the right thing to do. The last two weeks had turned her life upside down. She could deal with all the turns. But Cody, what about him?

Downing the last of the tea, she stood up, went into the kitchen and put her cup in the sink. She dismissed the need to nose around. As much as she wanted to know where his wife was she didn't want to experience his wrath.

Wandering back into the living room, she eyed the pictures on the mantel. The little girl in the photos looked just like Mick. There wasn't any doubt about her parentage. The piece of metal she'd been forbidden to touch lay on the end of the mantel, daring her.

Kate glanced over her shoulder. Any minute he could appear and jump on her, but he was in the other room hooking up the Nintendo for Cody.

She moved to the end of the mantel. Her hand shook as she reached for the piece. Gently, she picked it up. It was an odd thing to have displayed. Kate turned it over. A piece of grillwork. It had come from the right side of a car, she was sure. The tiny ridge of cast material on one side hadn't been ground away. She thumped the piece with her finger. It was an alloy. Foreign. Bouncing it in her hand, she gauged its weight.

"What are you doing?"

Mick's razor-sharp question sliced through her concentration. Caught off guard, she whirled around. "I'm...I'm..." She closed her hand around the metal and held her hands behind her back. "I'm enjoying the fire."

He stalked toward her.

Overwhelmed by the desire to run, she stood her ground as his gaze slid down the mantel, stopped and came back to her.

"Where is it?"

She brought her hand out from behind her back and opened it. The metallic scrap lay in her open palm. "What is it, Mick?"

"You tell me." He locked an inquisitive stare on her.

It made her uncomfortable, but she stared right back at him, watching his jaw flex as he worked his teeth against each other.

His stance, hands on his hips, warned her she'd crossed some invisible line.

She swallowed the lump that formed in her throat. "It's a piece of grillwork. From the feel of it, it's from a foreign model, probably a mid to late nineteen-ninety." She looked at the piece again. "A Porsche maybe."

Mick's hands dropped from his hips. She saw him suck in a deep breath and let it out. His face went pale and he deflated like a leaky balloon. He took the grillwork out of her hand and laid it back on the mantel.

"You expect me to believe you know all of that, just by toying with it?"

He plopped down on the sofa and rubbed his hands up and down his face before he looked at her again.

"Yeah."

"Give me one reason why I should believe you."

Guilt tied her tongue. "Fine. It's just a piece of metal. Maybe it's your idea of a knickknack. Maybe it's a paperweight. How the heck should I know?"

"Whoa." He stood up suddenly. "You started this, Kate. Do you have the facts to back it up?"

She felt hot all over. If she told Mick how she'd obtained the knowledge, she was sure he'd think less of her, and she'd been working really hard to convince him she wasn't a car thief anymore. "I'm pleading the fifth."

"No way." He was beside her. "If you know the kind of car it came from, you better tell me how you got that information."

The plea in his pale green eyes bordered on desperation. Why was the chunk of metal so important? "Where did you get it, Mick?"

He moved slowly around her. "Come on, you know where I got it. You know everything about it…don't you?"

The accusatory tone in his voice bristled her nerves. His body language screamed menace. She stepped back. Caution surged in her veins and built like a riptide. "No."

He clamped his hands onto her forearms. An electrical current jolted into her body, made her heart race. "Stop it, Mick. Stop it. What's wrong with you?"

Releasing her, he stepped back. The fire in his eyes cooled and he sat back down on the sofa. Confusion swirled in her mind, stirred by his odd behavior.

Mick leaned into the sofa cushions, in need of a comfortable place to fall. If Kate knew anything about the accident, she was good at hiding it. From the top of her head to the tip of her toes, she appeared to be honest.

"Enough. We'll talk about it later." He stood up, drained. For years he'd wanted to know what had really happened to his wife and daughter. Now he wanted to talk about it later?

He pushed past her and went into the kitchen, but she followed him. Her expression was curious, determined. He wanted to hold out on her, but she wasn't going to let him.

"Tell me about them."

"They're dead. Killed in an accident." He turned away, turned against the sympathy that lined her beautiful face. He didn't want to see her pity. He wanted her to give him the answers he'd waited years for.

Which Robear killed his family? Who was he going to kill with his bare hands? Just a name and he could rest.

Her hand on his back made him jump and tipped his nerves on end. He was shocked by the desire her gesture aroused. Slowly he turned around, prepared to start with her, but he hesitated, studying the sorrow in her eyes, the apology on her lips.

Her lips. Caught in a torrential passion he couldn't control, he moved against her and pinned her to the counter with his body. Like a landslide, his desire buried doubt and he moved to take her. She was a beautiful woman and he was hungry, hungry to feel her beneath him, hungry for a closeness he needed to share.

If only she weren't a material witness. If only he weren't a cop sworn to duty. His desire crashed. She could have been driving the car that killed Natalie and Megan for all he knew. Maybe that's how she'd known the model of the car's grillwork. She was behind the wheel that night.

"I'm sorry." He leaned against the counter, watching the rapid rise and fall of her chest as she regained her composure. She'd felt it, too?

"I'm out of line."

"Me, too." She started to fiddle with the dish towel on the counter. Her hand shook as she fingered the terry cloth. "Listen, I've been thinking about our situation." She raised coffee-colored eyes to his and he felt the earth move. "I'm going to take Cody to my family for protection, but I'm going to stay with you."

A jumble of thoughts bounced around in his mind. She was going to stay with him?

"I can't let you do that, Kate. If there's a safe place to hide, you belong there, too."

"You don't have a choice. My name was on the windshield. I'm safer with you and we can lead them away from Cody. Oak Wood has an impenetrable security system."

He held up his hand to silence her. In her position he'd probably do the same thing. Maybe she was correct. They could do a better job. "I understand."

"It's nothing personal." She moved to touch his arm but he pulled away to dodge the physical bullet he was in no condition to take at the moment. Kate was dangerous. Touching her was even more dangerous, but she'd just agreed to accept his protection.

"I'll clear it with my supervisor." Mick left the room, a strange new hope in his gut. He was about to enter the Robear twilight zone. Keeping Kate close was going to pay off as he'd never imagined. She could take him deep into a world he'd only skirted.

She was his ticket in.

MICK FOCUSED ON THE ROAD in front of him. It would be like the Robears to hide as far away from the law as they could. That explained their tendency to be everywhere and nowhere at the same time. Was this place even on the map?

"Turn here." Kate's voice was loaded with tension. Why was she so afraid to speak with her family?

The sound of the tires leaving pavement and crushing gravel put a knot in his stomach. Without Kate in the seat next to him, he doubted he'd ever find his way out of these parts. The road narrowed and turned to washboard, jittering the car to a crawl.

The headlights pushed into the darkness, but he couldn't see beyond their scope. The vegetation was dense. Saplings and branches from taller trees raked the sides of the car. Even if he stopped, there was nowhere to turn around.

The road went on forever and became tighter the farther they advanced. Even the leaf canopy overhead appeared to reach down and smother them.

"Where are we, Kate?"

"A little farther."

Mick held his uneasiness at bay and focused ahead. He'd have to trust her.

A solid wall of vegetation loomed in front of them. It had to be ten feet tall. He took his foot off the gas and braked, hard. "What the…"

"Pull forward. Touch the nose of the car to it."

"This is nuts." Out of habit, Mick looked into his rearview mirror. How was he going to back the car out of this hole? He'd always been a believer in what he saw and what he saw was an impenetrable wall in front of them.

"Just do it." Her voice went high. The dash lights illuminated a wet trail down her cheek. She wiped it away.

"What's up, Kate? You know we don't have to do this. There are other ways."

"Not safe ones. This isn't about me anyway. It's about Cody. They can protect him. I can't."

Guilt burned through him. He hadn't been able to keep Kate or Cody safe, either. It was going to take criminals to do it?

"Where do you want to go? How far?"

She reached out in the darkness and touched his leg, sending a firestorm through his body.

"Here."

"Okay." He edged the car forward until it touched the wall of green.

"A little more."

"That's it. Anymore and we'll…" The green wall moved, giving against the bumper of the car. It opened to the left in one giant sweep. "A gate?"

"Yeah, but once you pull through, get ready."

"For what."

"My big brother. He knew we were coming twenty minutes ago."

He stepped down on the gas pedal and squeezed the car through the opening. They'd no more than emerged on the other side when a man stepped into the beam of the headlights.

Mick braked, the hair bristled on his neck as he stared down the barrel of a twelve-gauge shotgun.

Chapter Six

Kate rolled down the window, "Frank!"

"Kate. Is that you?"

"It's me."

She opened the car door and stepped out, overwhelmed with a warmth she hadn't felt in years. Frank, her oldest brother, seemed taller.

He laid the shotgun across the hood of the car, scooped her into his arms and spun her in a circle. "Where have you been?"

"Around, Frankie. Just around." Relief spread through her, her heart flexed in her chest and she released a swell of tears.

"Mom's going to be glad to see you. She hasn't been well." He set her down.

She gave Frank a shake of her head, warning him they weren't alone. "I want you to meet my…boyfriend." She couldn't believe what she'd just said, but if Mick wanted to fit in he needed a cover.

Frank leaned in the door and shook Mick's hand. "Nice to meet you."

"You, too."

It had been years since she'd talked to Frank. She could only hope he and Mick hadn't crossed paths before tonight.

"Come up to the house."

"Jump in."

Frank opened the back door, set to get in the car, but stopped when Cody sat up. "Mommy, where are we?"

Her nerves stretched. "Scoot over and let your Uncle Frank in."

"Uncle Frank?" He obeyed and slid into the center of the seat.

"Why didn't you tell us, Kate?"

"I wanted to. It just got easier to leave it unsaid, then the accident…"

Mick felt like a kid eavesdropping from behind the curtain. *Accident? What accident?* Were they talking about Natalie and Megan? Curiosity seared a trail from his mind to his heart. How was Kate involved? Was she so repulsed by what her family had done she'd disowned them? He shifted in his seat, wanting to take Frank Robear apart piece by piece to get the truth, but he needed evidence or a confession. Solid proof they were involved in the hit-and-run. Legalities cooled his hot head. He'd bide his time until they confessed. This was the perfect spot to be in.

Frank closed the car door and Mick edged forward, glad when the road opened up and turned to blacktop. It was a contrast he hadn't expected. The more he knew about them the less sense it made. A family of car thieves in the middle of nowhere, a secret entrance into their lair... What next?

They rounded the corner and he stopped the car. Like a throwback to medieval times, a massive stone house sat perched on a small knoll. Warm light glowed from tall windows, inviting him in, in a strange and intriguing way.

"Wow." He let the word slip out and stepped on the gas. He knew they'd been successful, but this was success times ten. The car lights swept past neatly shaped trees and chopped grass.

"What do you think?" Kate asked.

He shot a glance her way, but he couldn't be honest with her. Dirty money still spent. "Great place." He pulled up in front of the house and shut off the engine. "Who lives here?"

"My mom and Frank." Kate opened the door

and stepped out of the car, stretched and opened the back door. "Come on, Cody. It's time to meet your grandma Robear. I think you'll like her."

Cody scrambled out after Frank and took his mother's hand.

Mick zoomed in on Kate's expression in the glow of the gargantuan light fixtures on either side of a double-doored stone archway. She stood very still. He saw her shoulders rise and fall along with her breath, as if entering would signify some sort of surrender. What war raged inside of her? What secrets kept her rooted to the spot, afraid to enter and afraid not to?

"Come on, Kate. It's cool out here. Let's go inside." Taking her hand, he led her up the steps to the front door.

Frank moved around them and bumped into Mick. "Sorry. I always miss that top stair."

"No problem."

He made the landing and opened the door. "Mom." His voice echoed against the high ceiling of the foyer.

Mick led Kate and Cody over the threshold and closed the door. A clap like thunder echoed through the house. He felt as if he'd been pushed into the past. They'd stepped into a sixteenth-century fortress equipped with twenty-first-century stuff. Creepy.

"You'll have to excuse my mother, she has a flair for drama. She wants to scare you with a first impression you'll never forget, but she's harmless."

Cody moved behind Kate, wrapped his arms around one of her legs and peered out at the massive interior of the home, fixated on the full suit of armor next to a narrow trestle table.

Mick smiled down at him hoping to offer some assurance that everything was cool. There weren't any black knights behind the potted plants ready to ambush them.

"Mom, it's Katie. She's here." Frank moved into the great room.

From the back of the house a clatter of glass smashing against the tile set Mick's nerves on edge.

"Come on, Kate. Mom's not doing well."

"What do you mean, not well?"

Mick heard Kate's soft cry and resisted the desire to comfort her.

"She has Alzheimer's. Early stages."

Cody suddenly changed alliances and wrapped his arms around Mick's leg. His eyes grew to the size of silver dollars as he stared up at Mick.

Mick scooped him up and felt the child relax in his arms once they moved past the armor.

They followed Frank and Kate down a long hallway with rooms off both sides. It emptied into a large family room. The kitchen was on the right.

He heard Kate sigh and watched her approach a tall woman who leaned against the kitchen counter, her face in her hands.

"Mama?" Kate moved toward her mother, unsure of her mood. She never knew how Geneva Robear would react. She'd given up on second guesses a long time ago. Hundreds of glass shards surrounded her mother and she tried to remember where the broom was.

In surreal time, Geneva raised her face, her eyes transfixed. "Kate?"

"Yes, Mom. It's me." She blinked back the tears just behind her lids. "I've come to ask you for help."

Geneva's expression was stony. Not even Alzheimer's had ground away the edge of disapproval that always seemed to be there.

"You left this house on your own. And when you did, you left my protection."

"I know." She stepped closer, ignoring the crunch of glass under the soles of her shoes. "I wouldn't ask for myself. I'm asking for someone else…my son. Your grandson."

Her mom put her hand to her chest, as if her

heart was swelling underneath it. She clutched her pink silk blouse, a small sigh escaped between her thin lips. "Grandson?"

"His name is Cody. He's four." Kate moved closer, craving her mother's arms.

"Four," Geneva whispered the word. Her eyes caught fire as realization smacked her brain. "Jake?"

"Yes, Mom. Jake's son needs your protection. Will you help him?"

She fidgeted under her mom's glare of disapproval. She'd always hated Jake Talbot, had warned her to stay away from him.

"Where is the boy?"

"Cody." Turning to look at them, her gaze met Mick's straight on. Did she see sympathy in the green depths?

Mick set him down and offered quiet reassurance. The gesture warmed her from the inside out.

"Come and meet your grandma."

With timid steps, Cody came to her side. "Mom, this is Cody."

Geneva held out her hand.

"Go ahead." A zing of satisfaction went through her as Cody put his small hand into Geneva's hand. Generations together. As it should be.

"How do you do, Cody?"

A smile spread over his lips. In that instant, she knew he would be fine. Geneva was a gruff woman, but behind her dark eyes there was kindness.

"What do you say, I show you where the cookie jar is?"

"Yeah."

"Right there." She swept her hand toward the counter and a ceramic jar shaped like an apple.

Cody moved to the counter and put his hands on the edge. He raised onto his tiptoes and reached for the jar, but he was too short.

Kate caught her mother's expression out of the corner of her eye. She wore a curious smile, one that rivaled the Mona Lisa.

Looking around the kitchen, Cody spied a step stool in the corner. He went to it and patted the seat, then dragged it over to the counter and climbed onto it. Easily he opened the jar and reached inside to pull out a handful of Oreo cookies. Sitting down, he happily bit into one.

"Looks like he can stay, Kate. He's a lot like you."

"Yes, he is." She looked at her beautiful son, so proud he'd accomplished the task. Ingenuity had always been a prized Robearian trait. "I need you and Frank to watch over him…raise him, if I don't come back." Reality settled in her mind. He would be safe here.

In a matter of minutes, Geneva Robear had undone four years of hard work. Four years of trying to distance herself from her family and their illegal activities. Now she was here, standing in her mother's kitchen asking her to protect him, but if anyone could do it, she could.

Her heart broke like the Oreo cookies Cody bit into. She was going to have to leave him here. Leave him in the very environment she was trying to escape. A hint of doubt crept into her mind. Maybe she should reconsider.

"He'll be fine."

Frank's voice cut into her thoughts and pushed her decision back in the other direction. She'd always been able to rely on him. He'd always been there. A stalwart advocate, even against Geneva.

"I know."

Mick watched them. His eyes sharp, interested. Somehow she'd have to keep him at a distance. "We need to go. I can't tell you much—" she pulled out a card "—but here's my cell number if there's a problem and my e-mail address." Her chest tightened around the next question she had to ask. "Is Dylan doing his thing in old town?"

Frank's eyes narrowed. "What do you want with Dylan? You should steer clear of him."

"I need to talk to him. Just tell me if he's still over on Wilson."

"Yeah. Same old, same old. Watch your back. Things have changed since the accident." Frank leaned against the counter. "Does he know about Cody?"

"No."

"He's blood, Kate. It's thick."

"I know. Maybe someday."

Mick had moved in beside them and leaned nonchalantly against the counter, mirroring Frank's easy mood, but she could see him soak up the words of their conversation in cop fashion. Her past was none of his business and she intended to keep it that way.

"We've got to go. Right Mick?"

He turned a lazy green gaze on her. "Sure thing, doll."

She looked away, overwhelmed by the sexy warmth in his voice. The heat of desire crept up her neck. Mick Jacoby was dangerous in more ways than one.

"Just let me tell Cody goodbye."

"No problem."

Kate moved to where Cody protected his pile of cookies. "Share?"

"Okay, but Grandma said I can have all I want."

"Yeah. I say you can have six, that's it, and brush those teeth before bed."

"Ah," he mumbled with his mouth full.

"Give me a hug and don't drive your grandma and Uncle Frank crazy."

"Okay." He smiled, showing Oreo-stained baby teeth.

Kate held him close, but holding him didn't feel like enough. She had to be strong. Had to think of him first.

"Kate, is that you?"

"Yeah, it's me." She took a chance, released Cody and moved toward her mom.

"How have you been, dear?"

She put her arms around her mother and hugged her tight. "Good."

Geneva patted her back. "Do you want a cookie?"

"No thanks." She stepped back.

"Suit yourself." Geneva put her hand into the cookie jar and pulled out a macaroon. She bit into it, eyeing Cody with curiosity. "Who are you?"

Cody glanced up at his grandma and smiled.

"Don't worry. He'll be fine. Oak Wood has only gotten better with age, just like me."

She hugged her brother. "What about her?"

"Time. She's in the midstage of the disease, her short-term memory is gone, but it's different for every person who gets it."

Mick moved in next to her and took her hand. "Gotta go. It's late."

She waved goodbye and followed him out of the house. The night had grown cold and the smell of rain hung in the air. She wanted it to pour. Nothing like spring rain to wash her emotions away. Her world was inside that house. Safe, but no longer a physical part of her. She ignored the sadness she felt leak into her bloodstream. His safety was more important than a temporary bout of separation anxiety.

It was the right thing to bring him here. Few people knew about the place, still fewer would ever reveal its location. She could focus now. Focus on what lay ahead.

"Kate…Kate." Mick's voice interrupted her tangled thoughts.

"It'll be okay." He lifted her chin with his fingers. His warmth and closeness settled her apprehension. "I know what you just did is eating you alive, but he's safe. Safer than I could have ever made him. I want you to know he'll be home soon. We'll catch these guys. I promise."

Mick's eyes were alive with an intense glimmer. Determination, she guessed. It's what made him magnetic. Made him different from most men she'd met, but something about Mick Jacoby kept them together. Something strong. Was it need? Did she need him? Yes, she decided. Very aware of his fingers against her skin.

"Let's get out of here." Mick had the urge to move. Restless energy festered inside of him. He was moving closer to the truth.

He took her hand and walked her to the car, ignoring the comfortable fit that existed between them.

He opened Kate's door and closed it after her. Taking one more look at the fortress she'd called home, he climbed in and pulled away.

The green gate worked the same way from the inside and he was determined to remember how to get to the house.

"Where to?"

"Wherever you want to go. I'm too tired to care."

"We'll get a room."

"Okay."

Silence fell between them and he got into the hypnotic rhythm of the road underneath the tires, but before he had time to get his next move planned, they were at a junction.

"Were you going to ask me for directions, or would that bruise your ego?"

Her question was humorous, but true. He still had no idea where they were.

"Go left."

He turned left, trying to mentally plot the route they'd taken, but things didn't looked familiar. It felt like one giant circle. Frustration burrowed just below the surface, ready to break through any moment.

"Go right."

They turned onto a narrow dirt road and crept along until he could see the back-and-forth movement of cars in front of him. A major highway?

"Go right."

"Where are we, Kate?"

"I'm not going to tell you. I won't betray my family. You think I'm not always aware you're a cop? You think you can flash those luscious green eyes, smile, and I'll spill my guts?"

He was uncomfortable, as if he'd been turned inside out. All his years of police training tossed out by a beautiful ex-car thief? He was seriously slipping.

"I'm just doing my job. If I don't look at everyone as a suspect, I'm likely to miss something."

"My family is clean. They don't have anything to do with Otis Whittley."

"And you know that for sure?"

"No, I don't. But it's not their style. The Robears have a tried and true way of doing things. They'd never resort to murder."

"Really?" He bit back the accusation he'd been about to fling and took a deep breath. Kate was his pigeon. He couldn't blow it in a fit of ego. "Look, Kate. I need you. You're a material witness under my protection. You can trust me."

He searched her face in the dimly lit interior of the car, hoping for confirmation that he'd soothed her anger, but she glared at him.

"Trust you? Don't think for one second I don't know what you're up to. I won't let you attack my family." She crossed her arms and sat back.

Mick took his frustration out on the gas pedal. The car shot onto the highway, tires spinning, gravel flying. Arguing with her was taxing. He'd accused her of holding out. But was she?

His heart told him no, but he'd mentally been holding onto the Robears. Until that could be proven wrong, he planned to go on believing they'd killed his wife and daughter. He gathered his emotions together and bundled them. He'd have to put his game face on if he wanted the information Kate had.

"I'm sorry for pushing. I've been doing it for so long, I don't know what else to do." He chanced a sideways glance at her. Her body language had changed. She'd relaxed against the seat, head back, eyes closed. Asleep?

The highway stretched in front of him and a Motel 6 sign loomed in the distance. He was bone tired himself. Brain tired, too. He pulled into the parking lot and shut off the car. His guess put them somewhere on the north side of New Orleans, but he wasn't sure. He couldn't even report where they'd just been. His superior would think he had air for brains when he gave him the details. Mick sighed and climbed out of the unit. They'd get a room for the night and he'd reclaim his bearings in the morning.

The overhead bell on the office door dinged as he pushed into the lobby. A woman sat behind the desk watching a small TV.

"Hello." He moved up to the front desk. "I need a room. Two beds, please."

"We're full."

"Full?" He hadn't noticed many cars in the parking lot.

"You sure about that?"

"Yep. There's another place about a mile down the road. You could stop there."

"I could. Have you got a room with one bed?"

She looked up at him over heavy-rimmed glasses. "Sure. Why didn't you say so in the first place?"

Stifling a you've-got-to-be-kidding grunt, he scribbled info on the card she handed him. He wasn't sure how Kate was going to take the one bed information. "I need some extra blankets."

She stood up and pushed through a swinging door into the back room. A moment later she reappeared with an armload of bedding. "Here you go." She plopped the blankets onto the counter. "Will that be cash or credit?"

"Cash."

"I need to see your driver's license."

Mick pulled his wallet out of his pocket and opened it. His license wasn't staring up at him from its usual place inside the plastic cover. "What the...?" Someone had removed it and put it behind his credit cards. He'd been made by Frank Robear?

"Sorry." He pulled out some cash and paid the bill.

"Your key. It's room 32. Out the door, up the stairs and right."

Mick picked up the blankets and the key. "Thanks."

She'd already turned back to the tiny images on-screen.

The bell on the door sounded as he pushed out into the night. He'd open the room before he woke Kate up. Climbing the steps, he glanced down at the car.

"Damn." Mick dropped the blankets, charged down the stairs and flung the passenger's side door open.

The car was empty.

Kate was gone.

Chapter Seven

Kate climbed out of the cab. The old neighborhood looked the same, but smaller than she remembered it, older. The sidewalks were crumbling, the commercial buildings all in need of fresh paint to cover time's march forward. Maybe she was the one who'd changed. She'd grown up.

Tamping down a wave of panic, she stared at Dylan's shop across the street. She hadn't spoken to him in years. Not since Mercy Hospital, the night of Jake's car accident where his emotions had boiled over.

She put her backpack on her shoulder and stepped into the street. It was hard to imagine bringing Mick along on this mission, but ditching him hadn't been easy. Thank goodness Frank had picked her up after she gave him the slip. They'd had eight hours to catch up on five years' worth of living.

Putting one foot in front of the other, she crossed the street. It was going to be tough to face Dylan Talbot. Maybe time had cooled his anger.

A number of cars were parked in the front lot. Both the garage doors were down, but an open sign sat in the window next to the front door.

She strolled across the parking lot and entered the front office. A blast of AC worked to cool her cheeks, but it couldn't fix the pucker of nervousness in her stomach. She glanced around the familiar office and read the sign that hung over the front counter, OUR CREDIT MANAGER IS HELEN WAIT, SO IF YOU WANT CREDIT, GO TO HELL'N WAIT.

Through the glass in the connecting door she could see a man work his way back and forth between his toolbox and a car with its hood up. Dylan Talbot.

Kate took a breath, remembering the nights she'd helped Dylan and Jake take a car down in two hours. Cars she'd stolen. Undoing the tangle of emotions tying her in knots, she pushed open the door.

Her legs shook as she moved toward him. She swallowed, rehearsing the words she'd worked over, but her mind went blank when he rose and stared at her.

She stopped. Frozen to the floor.

Dylan rubbed his greasy hands on a rag hanging out of his coveralls' pocket. "What do you want? I'm busy."

"I can see that." Sweat leached onto her palms. "I'm sorry for what happened to Jake. I had no idea he'd take my dare. I would have stopped him…."

In three steps he was on her, his fingers digging into the flesh of her upper arms. "The hell you would of! You egged him on. You pushed him because he loved you. Jakie would have done anything for you, Kate. You're nothing but a tease." He pushed her.

She stumbled backward from the force, her balance challenged by his shove. She hit something solid. Something human. *Mick Jacoby.*

"Hey, man, don't push my babe around."

He held her tight against him. She relaxed, a surge of relief moving inside her coupled with the tingle of tension his closeness sparked.

"Who the hell are you?" Dylan asked, his stance loaded with menace. He pushed his sleeves up and prepared for a fight.

Mick tensed against her. The butt of his gun pressed into her side. Concern zipped through her.

"Mick. Mick Jackson. Kate here says you're

the best takedown artist in New Orleans. That true?"

Dylan's attitude changed. He put his hands on his hips and stared straight at Mick. Dylan had never been one to pass up the opportunity to juice up his bank account. Mick had him pegged.

"Suppose I am. What do you have in mind?"

"I've got a couple of high-end Beamers coming in next week with a dude named Otis. I'd like 'em cut and wrapped in, say…a weekend. Can you handle it?"

Dylan's cocky half smile faded like an old Polaroid. "Not interested."

"What difference does five seconds make?" Mick nudged Kate aside and stepped toward Dylan.

Dylan shot a glance at her and looked back at Mick.

"He's cool," she insisted. He'd always trusted her in business deals, just not with his baby brother.

"Look." Dylan ran the grease rag over a wrench. Not even the constant movement could hide the tremble of his hands. Dylan Talbot was scared? Kate focused on his face. She'd never seen him like this.

"Otis is tight with some nasty people. I don't

want any trouble. I take things down, that's it. Details aren't for me." He laid the polished tool on the radiator of the car. "You should back off. Guys in his circle stop breathing."

"If you know something, spill it. I don't want any trouble, I like air. If I need to ditch my transaction, it's cool."

Dylan looked around and swallowed. "Otis is mixed up with some wicked dude. Word on the street is, the contact is a cop, or something."

"Are we talking rides?"

"Yeah, but they're special. I don't know what kind of trade they're running, but I like the smell of smuggling."

"Maybe I better end our association. There are lots of other grabs out there and a flashy car on every corner."

"I would. Hey, if you need a takedown from anyone but Otis, let me know." Dylan nodded toward Kate. "You seen Jake lately?"

Kate internally squirmed underneath the question. Mick was looking at her now, waiting. "A couple of weeks ago."

"I haven't been over to see him. Those places give me the creeps."

"Me, too." She took Mick's hand and gave it a tug in an attempt to signal it was time to leave, but he didn't budge.

"Jake? Who's Jake?"

A fever flared inside of her, pushed out by fear. Fear that her secret would be opened like a book, that Mick would be able to read it aloud, condemn her as she condemned herself.

"My brother…Jake's my brother." Dylan cast a hard look at her, turned back to the car and ducked his head under the hood. "If you want details, ask her."

She was thankful for the slim measure of honor Dylan had shown. No one wanted to hear stories about their girlfriend from someone else.

Mick was on the move. He took her hand as they left the shop. By the time he got her to his car, his grip had tightened until her fingers stung.

He pinned her against the driver's side door with his body. "What's wrong with you, Kate? You think you can ditch me and go this one alone?"

"How'd you find me?"

"Good investigative skills and ears like a wolf. I heard you ask Frank about Dylan."

"I'll have to whisper next time." She tried to relax with the full frontal feel of his body against hers, but it was impossible. He was too close, too intense. She looked away from his hot green stare, but he pulled her chin back into alignment with his fingers.

"You heard what he said. Whittley's mixed up with some bad people. We've already had a taste of what they like to dish out. Do you think they'd mind killing you?"

She sucked in a deep breath and tried to avoid giving in to the surge of desire working its way through her body, only to pool just below her waist. "I have a history with Dylan. I didn't want to talk to him with you breathing down my neck. It's not a crime. I'm not your prisoner."

His expression hardened. He looked at her in a strange way. Somewhere between focused and fuzzy. Her words seemed to bounce off him, as he stared at her lips then back into her eyes.

Kate heard the front door of the shop slam shut and saw Dylan pause outside to watch them from across the street.

"Keep your voice down." Mick gave him a sideways glance and lowered his mouth to hers. "It's showtime."

Realization hit her at the same time their lips met. Lust burned into her and heated her body to white-hot. She put her arms around his neck and arched against him, eliciting a moan from deep in his throat. Her body hummed as he parted her lips with his tongue.

She tried to control her breathing, but she was out of control.

Mick pulled back too soon and she felt him shudder. His eyes glowed with surprise. She watched him swallow and run his hand over his head. Over his right shoulder, she saw Dylan go back inside, heard the decisive slam of the door.

"Damn, woman. You make me crazy." He stepped back from her as if distance would somehow help him regain control. "I hope he bought it, because in my line of work phony will get you dead. Is that what you want?"

She didn't want dead. Not when Mick had just made her realize how alive she was. "I want to get these guys. I want to go and pick up my son and I want the world to forget I'm a Robear…I want you to forget."

Like a cloud passing across the sun, his face darkened. "It's not that simple. You have no idea what the Robears took from me."

Anger squeezed her insides and the words spilled out. "Then why don't you tell me, Mick Jacoby, tough cop? What have you got against me, besides a junkyard of old car parts? I've never done anything to you."

The outburst jolted him, but his expression remained fixed. "What do you know about an accident on the north end May 10, 2000…a hit-and-run that killed a woman and a little girl?"

"Is this some sort of interrogation?" She swallowed.

"Just answer the question." His face went pale. He looked thirty-two times two, and she resisted the need to touch him, then the force of his question slammed into her, head-on. Mentally she repeated the date seared into her mind, forever. Her hand went to her mouth to cover the horror she felt leak from her bones.

Mick's hands were on her forearms. She could feel him tremble. Feel a flood of emotion rack his body, but his face was placid, flat. "You do know something!" He shook her. "Don't deny it, Kate. Tell me."

"That's why you won't leave me alone. You think I had something to do with your wife's and daughter's deaths? That's what this is about. You suspect me?" She searched his face for clues, a glimmer of recognition. Did he know she'd been there that night?

His eyes turned bottle-green as if going over the memory required a dive into deeper water. "Word hit the street right after it happened. The rumble incriminated the Robears in a boost that night. I've been after them ever since." He blinked several times and released her.

"They're ghosts, phantoms, smoke. Then I

found you in the storage unit and I knew for the first time I had someone who could lead me to the person who ran them down. You don't know what it's like to spend your life in a fight for justice. Wanting it so bad you wear it like skin. I finally had a flesh-and-blood Robear."

His confession jabbed into her heart and left it to bleed. She wanted to run, run as far away as she could. Run from the pain he exuded, pain that mirrored her own. Guilt was tying them together, carefully laced knots that trapped them both in threads of the past.

She reached for him, hesitantly, not sure if he would come, but he did. His arms went around her and he buried his face in her hair.

Her throat tightened with emotion and she closed her eyes against the flow of tears. She comforted him, as she would Cody. An injured boy in a man's skin. Battered by loss, changed by life. She had to help him. She had to prove him wrong. Could someone in her family drive over two people and live with themselves?

"I'll help you, Mick. I'll do whatever you want me to."

Mick pulled back and searched her face for the truth. His emotions were rubbed raw by the honesty he read in her expression, the slight crinkles at the corners of her eyes, the glow of moisture in them. His heart zigzagged and settled back into a calm rhythm.

At that moment he knew he could trust her, with his life if he had to. But nothing was free. He'd have to earn her trust in return. He'd have to level with her, no secrets.

"Why don't we start with that list of yours? I'd like to see the homes where you repoed the other cars. You never know what memory might be jarred if you return to the scene."

"Mick."

He looked into her upturned face. She'd managed to stir his emotions and climb under his skin. "Yeah."

"For what it's worth, I'm sorry."

He swallowed the lump in his throat. "Thanks."

"I'm going to ask Frank to check into it. I can't promise he'll turn anything up, but it's worth a try."

Tension built between his shoulder blades. "I don't want to know anything about how or where he gets the information. I'm sworn to uphold the law."

She squeezed his arm. "Fair enough."

He couldn't shake the feeling there was more she'd wanted to say. Her reaction to the date had been instantaneous. Given time, would she tell him what she knew about that night? "Let's get out of here."

"IS THIS THE PLACE?" Mick craned his neck and stared through the windshield at the big house in the middle of the Garden District.

"This is where I snagged Romaro's Mercedes."

"Let's have a look." He climbed out of the car and made the sidewalk before Kate had even opened the door.

She watched him move up the steps and felt a wave of spontaneous heat generate inside of her. He moved like a cat, like an exotic beast. Beautiful, primed and lethal, but for all his brawn, which she found really sexy, all his macho BS, it was his tender insides that made her heart twist in her chest.

"Looks empty." He stood on the front porch and peered into a window. "Not a stick of furniture. Just like my first apartment."

Kate put her runaway thoughts back on track and joined him on the porch. "The car was in the driveway." She pointed to the spot where the shiny red Mercedes convertible had sat, like a maraschino cherry on top of a banana split.

"Do you know who owns this place?" she

asked as she moved down the stairs and worked her way around to the back of the house.

"Don't know, but I'm going to find out. I'd like to tie all the repo sites to one person. He'll have a lot of explaining to do."

She tried the back door and was surprised when the knob turned in her hand.

"You've got a thing for unlocked doors, don't you?"

"I do what works."

They entered the rear of the house. A short hallway lined with storage cupboards opened into a large kitchen. The place was spotless. Too clean.

"Look at this." She spotted a business card on the counter near the sink. "It's a management company. Do you suppose they handle this property?"

"We'll see." He took the card and dialed the number on his cell phone. "Hi, I was wondering if you manage a property?" He rattled off the address and paused, casting a long slow look at her. "Great. Who does? I see. Thanks."

He ended the call and closed the phone. "She wasn't at liberty to disclose the information. We'll get a subpoena for the records. We'll look around, but I doubt there's any evidence of Romaro left in here. It's been scoured, probably rented since he used it."

They walked through the rest of the house, room by room. "I need this cleaning lady's number."

"You do okay."

"Thanks." He shot her a smile that showed straight white teeth and her emotions rocketed again.

"Let's go downtown. I've got to talk to Schneider. See what he's come up with."

"Do you think there's a link between Romaro and Otis, besides me?"

"One's dead, one's missing, presumed dead, and just to make it more interesting another deadbeat was caught in Michigan making a run for the Canadian border driving a two-hundred-fifty-thousand dollar Maserati, holding a suitcase full of cash."

"You're kidding?"

"Would I kid you?" He smiled a wicked smile. "Orlando Durant is fighting extradition back here for grand theft auto. What do you know about him?"

"Nothing really, but that's a name you don't forget." She scanned the list to refresh her memory. "It was a Jag. I think it was maroon. I took it in broad daylight over on Vivian."

"Do you remember anything unusual about him, the car or the house?"

"Have you ever seen a maroon car with pink seats?"

"Not exactly stock, huh?"

"Far from it. The rest of the interior was maroon leather, just the seats were different. They'd been replaced."

Mick looked at her and for an instant she saw the spin of his cop-wheeled brain. "That's it Kate. Smuggling, like Dylan said, but what was in those cars?"

"Drugs maybe? I don't know. All of the cars were imports."

"Did all the cars go to the same lender?"

"Yeah, Dallas Savings and Loan."

"What was the payoff on those repos, how much?"

"Five thousand, on delivery."

A small tic worked his jaw. "You never thought that was excessive?"

The angle of his question was sharp. Worse yet was the shame that hatched in her mind. "It occurred to me, but the paperwork was legit. How was I supposed to pass on that kind of money? I have Jake to take…" Her tangent had betrayed her, gotten the better of her ability to keep him secret, keep him tucked away, out of sight, out of mind.

"His name has come up a lot. Who is he?"

She couldn't escape Mick's searching gaze, couldn't run.

She swallowed the first words of denial that tried to get up her throat. "Cody's father. Dylan's brother. Jake Talbot."

"See, that wasn't so hard, was it. The only thing I can't understand is why you talk about him like he lives on the moon."

"He may as well." She fanned a heat wave of guilt. "He's in a nursing home. He's twenty-eight. A quadriplegic."

"What happened?"

"It was an accident, a rollover in a stolen car." A car she'd dared him to take. "He was ejected, suffered a broken neck and brain damage. He's on a respirator, unable to move. Messed up. It's the least I can do to pay the bills. That's why I need the money. I want him to have the best."

Mick felt a zing of jealousy zap him, then disappear. Kate was good; Jake was a lucky man to have her watching out for him. Loving him? Did she still?

"That's noble stuff." He moved down the steps, but he had the feeling there was more to her admission. The state could be picking up the tab. Why did she need to do it?

He opened the car door for her. "Let's roll past the rest of those addresses." They climbed into the car and Mick fired the engine. She was quiet sitting in the passenger seat. Revealing emotional baggage could take it out of you and he planned to give her lots of space. He couldn't get too close without getting involved.

"Why don't you work some of that Robear magic and see if you can find anything out about those pink seats?" He cast a sideways glance at her and pulled into traffic. "It's not exactly a desirable color unless you like Barbie and a greasy takedown artist wouldn't forget that anytime soon."

"You're right. I'll call Frank. He still has friends in the business who might remember."

"Still?"

"Yeah. I don't know if your fancy computers spit that piece of information out, but my brother is clean. He got his law degree six years ago. Well over the statute of limitations on grand theft auto."

Mick braked at an intersection and glanced in his rearview mirror. Several car lengths behind them trailed a black car with dark tinted windows.

The light changed, he stepped on the gas pedal and switched lanes just past the intersection. The black car followed.

"Sorry Kate. I can't stop being a cop just because you want me to."

"I don't want you to. I just want you to stop judging me and my family."

"Fair enough."

"Next stop, 4060 Lindstrom. Nathan Morris."

He turned right onto Beaux. The black car took the turn, but kept its distance.

"What make was the car you saw?"

"Honda. Why?"

"Flip down the vanity mirror."

She pulled down the visor and adjusted it so she could see out of the rear window. "That's it! That's the car."

Mick sped up and changed lanes, tracking the car on their tail in the rearview mirror. Kate was tense. He could see the stiffness in her shoulders. He reached out and touched her. "It'll be okay. We'll drag him around for a bit until we make him."

Working his way through town, he moved closer to the freeway and out of neighborhoods. There was no way to tell how aggressive the driver would get, or what he was willing to do to keep up.

Mick hammered the gas pedal and zinged onto I-10. The traffic was sparse and he pushed the V-6.

"I don't like this, Mick."

"I don't like it, either." He watched the little black car struggle to keep up. "Dispatch, 557."

"557, go ahead."

"I'm in need of a black-and-white. I'm being tailed by a late model, Honda Accord. Black. I'll try to get a plate number."

"Copy 557, unit 34 is southbound headed your way."

"Copy. Advise him to stay back."

"Affirmative."

Mick let off on the gas pedal. "Hang on, Kate, I'm going to reel him in, see if I can get a look at his plates."

She nibbled her lip and gave him a sideways glance. On the opposite side of the freeway a police car with its lights flashing pulled into the median and accelerated in behind the Honda.

Every passing second her heart rate climbed. What did the driver want? She glanced at the speedometer and held her breath. Mick was slowing down. Drawing the driver in.

"Here he comes."

In a split second the black car was on them. "Dispatch, 7638D as in…"

Mick's words ended abruptly. The rapid shift in gravity threw her forward. Metal on metal ground into her mind.

The tires squealed on the pavement. The impact of the forced collision jerked her body hard to the left.

"Hang on!"

Fear infused her; her pulse pounded in her ears. She fought to control the terror that jetted through her like lightning.

In slow motion, she looked over at Mick as the car spun and ground onto the shoulder. Dirt and gravel peeled over the windshield.

Mick's expression was intense as he tried to control the car to keep it from rolling.

In a flash it was over.

He didn't look at her until they'd come to an abrupt stop in a cloud of dust. "You okay?"

She sat up. "Yes."

The black-and-white sped by, siren blaring.

"You got the plate number?"

"Yeah."

A sob built in her throat, but she blinked back the tears.

"Dispatch. 557. Advise unit 34 to stand down. We got his plate number."

"Copy, 557."

She undid her seat belt and slid toward him. She wanted to feel safe. Wanted his arms around her.

He accepted her and pulled her against him, smoothed her hair away from her face with his fingers and whispered against her ear. "Someone wants to hurt you. I won't let it happen. I promise."

The jingle of his cell phone dispelled the moment and she found the courage to pull away.

"Jacoby.... When?" He continued to watch her as she settled into her seat and fastened her seat belt.

"I'll be right there." He closed his phone and put the car in gear. "They found Otis."

Chapter Eight

"Breathing?"

"No. You don't have to go with me. I can drop you at the station."

"I'm going. Where did they find him?"

"Bayou Gauche. Downriver a couple of miles from his place. A fisherman hooked into something, hauled it up and found him. He phoned it in."

Revulsion squeezed her stomach and she took a deep breath to drive it away. "I was the last one to see him alive."

"I was the last one to take one of his bullets."

Her heartbeat accelerated. Otis was dead. Probably killed by the same creeps who stalked her, broke into her house and tried to run them off the highway. She looked over at Mick, glad he was behind the wheel and not in the morgue.

"The hull marks on the bank behind the house make sense now. No wonder you didn't see any other cars on Bayou road. Otis was taken away in a small boat of some kind. They were right there. I could've had the SOBs."

"What are you, a frog?"

He smiled, but stared straight ahead.

"These guys are dangerous. I don't carry hip waders in my backpack. It wouldn't have been a smart move to go into the water after them. Besides, Otis was probably already dead when they put him in the boat."

"Maybe."

Mick's answer didn't make her feel better. What kind of animals did this stuff, and what kind of a man did it take to catch them? She considered him and her pulse thumped harder. She was physically safe with him next to her, but her heart was in trouble.

BAYOU GAUCHE LOOKED better in daylight, she decided as Mick maneuvered along the dirt road. Already the afternoon humidity warred with the car's air conditioner. She brushed her hair aside and tucked it behind her ear.

Mick braked for a slow-moving gator who'd chosen that moment to cross from one body of brackish water to the other. His tail swished back and forth as his short legs carried him forward.

She took a sideways glance at him and felt

her heart zing. She liked the truce they'd worked out. It was as good as invisible handcuffs, but not as tight. They both had everything to gain in a partnership and nothing to lose. Nothing to lose?

"Here we are." A long low whistle hissed from between his lips. "Looks like everyone made the party. There's a line at the punch bowl."

The narrow road was packed with police vehicles. The New Orleans's dive team milled around their van, still dressed in wet suits, tanks leaning against the tires. Uniformed cops wandered around while a man in a suit and tie stood with a notepad in hand talking to a man who was dressed in a fishing vest and a dorky hat, complete with fishing hooks hanging off it.

"What do ya know?"

She followed Mick's line of sight to a man who lounged against a bright yellow vintage Corvette. He looked at home in the circuslike commotion around him.

"Who is that?"

"My old partner from homicide."

Mick was already out of the car and striding toward him by the time she climbed out. Moving along, ten feet back, she took up a position near the divers' van within earshot of Mick and the guy who stood erect now, giving Mick a once-over.

"Jacoby, how the hell are you?"

"Not too shabby…yourself?"

"Good."

The guy he talked to seemed to mirror him. He was a head taller. His hair was dark, almost black. He looked past Mick and his gaze settled on her.

"Kate, come here," Mick called to her. "I'd like you to meet my buddy, Bret Byer. We grew up together."

A chill rippled across her skin and took refuge inside her. She looked away and tried to appear nonchalant, but when she looked up, he still stared at her. It was the slight smile on his lips that bothered her the most. It was the way she often looked at a hot fudge sundae, right before she devoured it, almost sexual in nature, definitely primal.

She extended her hand and he shook it vigorously.

"Jacoby, you've done it again. You always show up with the best-looking girl."

Mick caressed her with his gaze before he turned his attention to his friend.

"So what gets you out to Gauche?" He eyed Bret carefully. His ex-partner from the homicide division looked fit and leaned against a highly polished Corvette with a vanity plate that declared him, SMOOTH.

He processed all the details around the man in front of him. Customs had been a good move for him, lucrative, too, by the looks of it.

"I've got a little fishing pad over on the other side. Got word from my neighbor it had been broken into last night. I decided to come out and assess the damage. This guy—" he motioned to the fisherman deep in conversation with Investigator Callahan "—was walking along the road, pretty freaked out, I stopped to offer him a ride and he claimed he'd pulled up a body. We called the police. That was an hour ago and I'm still waiting to give my statement, then I'm out of here."

Mick nodded. "I'll see if we can get this expedited for you."

"No problem, buddy."

He turned his attention to Callahan as the CSI stalked toward him.

"There you are. Thought you'd like to have a look at the victim before we zip him in for a trip to the morgue. It's a fluke that Mr. Johnson found him at all." Callahan nodded to the fisherman next to him. "If we need more information we'll contact you."

The man turned and wandered away.

"Poor guy. Glad he didn't pull the victim into the boat, he'd be catatonic."

Mick grunted. "Yeah. So what can you tell me?"

Callahan motioned him in the direction of the coroner's van, four car lengths behind the dive-team vehicle. "The body is in bad shape. The gators gnawed on him, but we think it's Otis Whittley, at least that's the name on the ID we found in his wallet. Maybe you remember what the guy was wearing that night?"

"Flashy. He liked to party at the Alley-Gator." Mick thought about it. He'd watched Otis enter the club from across the street, but he'd been more interested in the location of the car than Otis's disco threads. Still, white bell-bottoms were unforgettable. "White pants. Dark jacket."

Callahan stopped at the rear of the van. "One more thing. He was cut up, looks like torture. Someone wanted something from him, I'd guess."

Just like Romaro.

Callahan opened the back of the van.

The stench of rotten flesh wafted to him and churned his stomach. "Rank."

"Wait until you see this." Callahan climbed in next to the gurney; Mick followed him. "Never seen anything like it. It wasn't done to kill the poor guy, either. It was done for effect. Probably post-morten." Callahan slid the zipper on the body bag and pulled it open. "Would you look at that?"

Mick stared at the ten-inch butcher knife buried in Otis's chest. "Straight through his breastbone." He recoiled.

"That's my guess."

"It'd take a lot of strength to pull that off." His nerves thinned. The assailants who'd done this were after Kate. He looked at the knife again. The lab would have to confirm what he already knew. The rosewood-handled butcher knife in Otis Whittley's chest belonged to Kate Robear.

"Looks like he's wearing bell-bottoms. Can't say they're white anymore, but yeah... that's him."

"We'll try to get something more in forensics. Say, isn't this the guy who owned that spicy BMW we picked up from storage?"

"Yeah."

"I went over that car. Found something of interest. It was fitted with LoJack. It wasn't stock. Someone installed it after the car hit the market. There was also an auxiliary alarm wired to the door switch, independent from the main system."

"Do you think this guy put them both in?" Mick nodded toward Otis, glad when Callahan zipped up the body bag.

"The auxiliary alarm, probably. I can check the components for his prints, but it was a hacked-in job. Amateur. The tracking device on the other hand, pro all the way. I'll check for prints, but I can almost guarantee there won't be any."

"Can you do me a favor, Callahan?"

"I can try."

Mick pulled out his pad and scribbled Kate's address on it. "There's a Bronco parked in the driveway at this address. Belongs to my material witness. Can you check it covertly this afternoon?"

"No problem." Callahan took the paper and shoved it into his pocket.

"Is there any way to find out if the slashed seats in the BMW were stock?"

"Yeah. I'll contact the manufacturer. They keep serial numbers on file for the car and all of its components."

"Thanks for the informative tour." Mick ducked his head and backed out of the van, taking a deep breath of fresh air.

"Sure thing. I'll stay in touch and get this guy's information down to Schneider, ASAP. I'll call you tonight."

"You're a good man." Mick moved around the corner of the van, glad he'd quit homicide.

He didn't have the stomach for it anymore. Not since…

The hair on his neck bristled and he battled a moment of irritation as he moved toward Kate and Byer. Kate's stance told him she wasn't enjoying Byer's advances. Her arms were crossed, her body turned; she was ready to run.

Byer stood close to her, too close. He leaned into the conversation, his hands in his front pockets, head cocked. A silent sexual invitation.

Mick slowed his pace and willed his testosterone level down. She wasn't returning the advance. He controlled the territorial lust that had swallowed him, brain and all. Kate was a beautiful woman. A beautiful woman he'd kissed. It aroused him just thinking about it. Crazy, but he had to give Byer credit for trying.

"Hey." He touched her arm and was rewarded with an instant zap deep into his body. "Ready to go?"

"Yeah. Nice to meet you."

"Likewise. Micky, let's get together for a beer."

"Sure."

Byer nodded and went back to his relaxed stance, just as Callahan approached him, notepad drawn.

Mick guided Kate to the car and climbed in

next to her, aware that Byer watched them with interest.

"What did Bret have to say?" He turned in the seat so he could look at her. Meter her reactions.

"Nothing really. He seemed to want to talk about you. Stuff like, how well I knew you. Had I known your wife? Did I want to get together? I haven't had a come-on that strong since my high school prom. I feel like I should go home and take a shower."

"He hit on you?"

"Yeah, wanted to take me to Pat O'Brien's for a Hurricane."

"He has a way with the ladies, but he gets his rocks off shuffling through them like a deck of cards. Don't let it upset you...he's harmless. I've trusted him with my life more than once."

Mick fired the engine, backed the car into a turnaround and pulled away from the scene.

"How'd you meet him?"

"We grew up together, high school, college and finally the academy. Fell in love with the same girl."

"How'd that work out?"

"I married her." He'd always admired the guy's style, but personally, he was a one-woman man. Casually, he slid a glance toward Kate. Content with the surge of emotion inside of him.

"Do they know how Otis died?"

Her question put him back in business, but he hesitated to answer her. He was sure Investigator Callahan would contact her soon enough. He'd added the knife to the break-in report and if he had to, he'd help him put two and two together. There was no way Kate had anything to do with it, but the police would want to know. "It'll be the coroner's call on the cause of death, but he was pretty messed up. Two weeks in the swamp can erase a lot of evidence."

"Like Romaro?"

"Same MO." He heard her heavy exhale and wondered about the knife. He knew he could trust her and he wanted her to trust him. "They found your knife in the body. The one missing from your house."

"In the body? No." She shook her head back and forth. "Are you sure it's mine?"

"Positive. It matches your set. Rosewood handle."

"They were in my house months ago? How do they know all the details of my life? I don't even know half the time where I'll be, or when. Are they clairvoyant? Mind readers? What?"

The color drained from her face, then surged back into her cheeks.

He flipped the AC on high. "I'm sorry, Kate. If I had the answers, I'd give them to you."

Highway 306 was in front of them and Mick braked. "We'll stay at my house tonight. We haven't been back there for days. I'll make sure we're not followed. I can make some dinner. Sound good?" He wanted to see the worry leave her face, wanted her to relax, if just for the night.

"Why, Officer Jacoby, I've never had an offer like that before. Are you trying to make it a date or take that kiss this afternoon to the next level?"

"No, ma'am. Just doing my job." Desire rattled him and sent his thoughts along paths that were better abandoned. As much as he wanted Kate, he knew it would compromise his investigation and his badge. It already had. He was acting like a stupid high school jock with the hots for the head cheerleader. More testosterone than brains.

"It's okay. I liked it, too."

"Don't encourage me. It's been a long time." He looked at her and she smiled. Mick pulled out onto the highway. She moved him. Stirred up emotional debris like a tornado across Texas.

"Look…Kate."

"I understand. You don't have to explain. I'm a witness, you're a cop assigned to protect me, not make love to me."

He couldn't tell her. Couldn't even begin to

understand it himself. He wanted her all right, but he owed closure to Natalie and Megan and that closure was sitting next to him. If he caved into lust, he'd risk the very thing that could end his five-year crusade.

Her.

"I HOPE YOU LIKE ITALIAN." Mick sat the grocery bag on the counter.

"Love it." Kate moved in and pulled the items from the bag.

"My wife, Natalie, was a great cook, but she never let me in the kitchen. I had to learn, or I'd have starved to death."

"Do you miss her?"

"Every day."

She reached over and touched his hand, driven by a need to console the man who'd lost so much. "Care to share?"

His eyes were bright under the overhead lights. "Come in here." He pulled away and left the kitchen.

She followed him into the living room, and knew where he was headed. He paused at the end of the mantel and picked up the chunk of metal.

"This is all I have from that night." He opened his palm to her. "It was the cleanest scene I've ever been to."

Horror washed over her. He'd been there and witnessed his dead family firsthand?

"No skid marks. No broken glass. No witnesses. Just some paint flakes the lab couldn't trace to a manufacturer and this chunk of nondescript metal. I found it the next morning in a storm drain across the street. I've had two labs go over it. Can you understand why I was skeptical when you examined it and declared it came from a Porsche?" Mick stared at the object in his hand. His face was placid, but his eyes sparkled with emotion.

"Yes." She moved to his side. She'd have to pick her way through a minefield of words. If she stepped on one, it was all over. "My family has taken down a lot of cars." She swallowed the admission almost as fast as she'd said it. It was acid in her mouth, the flavor of a lifestyle she'd come to hate. One she'd run from years ago. She was still running.

"I'm not proud of the way the Robears used to make a living, but I do know a piece of grillwork when I see one." She winced as he laid the metal back on the mantel and grasped her by her forearms. The intensity in his eyes threatened to melt her.

"Make me believe you. Can you do that?"

She matched his gaze with one of her own.

Could she tell him the truth? The rumor was true. There had been a Robear boost that night in his neighborhood. She knew the exact time, the exact street. She swallowed her doubt and raised her chin. "Yes."

Mick let her go and stepped back. He'd lost his freaking mind. He was going to trust her to tell him the truth? He looked at Natalie and Megan's pictures. It seemed like an eon since that night. The sharp edge had worn off of his pain and left only the need for closure. He could sleep now, but he'd sleep better when he caught their killer.

He looked at Kate's upturned face. Her sweet features highlighted with the look of innocence. "I'm going to hold you to it, but if you double-cross me, there won't be a place you can hide that I won't find you."

If he was frightening her, it didn't show. She looked back at him, unflinching, and he wanted to kiss her, but he held back. A tangled heart wasn't in his game plan. A tangled heart with a witness could never work.

"I planned to make dinner tonight. I better get on it."

She seemed disappointed when he stepped away from her and a slight degree of disappoint-ment invaded him. There was something magnetic about Kate Robear. Mick had to decide if it was her or the answers he was sure she had.

"What are you making?"

He stepped into the kitchen, aware of her behind him. "Lasagne."

Mick lifted the groceries out of the bag and Kate took over, shuttling them to the refrigerator. "I made lasagne once. You couldn't cut it with a chain saw. I must have overcooked it. All I had left was the garlic bread and the broiler got that. You should have seen the size of Cody's eyes when smoke rolled out of the oven. We had hot dogs for dinner."

He liked her sense of humor. Liked the sight of her in his kitchen. She caught him staring and stopped. The air around them came alive with electricity.

"Tell me about Cody's father." He knew he was digging too deep, shoveling too hard, but he had to know. Had to understand where they stood.

"We were never married. I got pregnant while we were engaged."

"Does that bother you?"

"It used to, but I've adjusted."

There was finality in her reply. Something he wished he'd been able to establish between himself and the past.

"Why didn't you marry him?" Curiosity took

over, leaving discretion a winded second. It was a great talent for a cop, but not so good in the relationship department.

"I almost did and then he was hurt in the accident. There was no going back."

"I understand." She licked her lips and fidgeted. There was more. What wasn't she telling him? He'd made her uncomfortable, of that he was sure.

"Did you love him?" His chest tightened and he wondered what it would be like to be loved by Kate Robear.

"As much as a young impressionable girl can love a macho good-looking male who thinks he's invincible."

"Fleeting?" he whispered, turning to her.

Kate could see the tension in Mick's shoulders. Was he jealous? She touched him. This time he didn't pull away but drew her into his arms.

"This is crazy." His hoarse admission in her ear was true. It was crazy that he held her, crazier still that she needed it as much as the air in the room.

He kissed her, gently at first, but the intensity increased until she parted her lips and let him explore her mouth with his tongue. He tasted sweet. She kissed him back, arched against him like a familiar lover.

From deep in his throat, he moaned. She could feel his arousal. Pleasure's fire burned through her, setting her ablaze.

Lifting her onto the edge of the counter, he slid his hands up the insides of her thighs. She opened for him and he leaned against her, kissed her neck and pulled her closer.

Inhaling his scent, she was caught up in the warmth of his touch, the strength in his body against hers.

Could she let this happen? Could she give herself to a man who despised her family? Did he hate her, too?

She pushed him back and took a labored breath. "We can't... I can't."

Mick's eyes were half-closed, clouded with need. He straightened and sobered, raking his fingers through his hair.

She watched him struggle against his body. He turned his back to her and left the kitchen. They had to catch whoever was responsible for the hit-and-run. Strip Mick's doubts. If they met up again, she didn't know if she'd stop him. She didn't want to, but it was the thought of him hating her, even while he made love to her, that she couldn't live with. She'd have to prove herself to him. Prove that she'd had nothing to do with the deaths. It wasn't going to be easy, but then nothing in her life had been.

Hopping down from the counter, she edged into the living room.

Mick put a match to the gas log in the fireplace and watched the flames come to life. He doubted there was anything short of the truth that could break the chill in his body. He watched her move into the room and sit down on the sofa, curling her legs beneath her. "How'd we get here, Kate?"

"By car?"

Normally he would have laughed at her silly answer, but tonight was serious. He'd kissed her for real. Felt her body against his.

"I don't know. Fate maybe? An extreme villain with a knife for a friend?"

Mick rubbed his hands over his face and moved to the chair opposite her. He couldn't get too close. Couldn't touch her again. "What if five years of hunting and three weeks of hell were all staged to bring us to this moment? You and me?" He swallowed and looked into her coffee-colored eyes.

"That's stupid. It's impossible." She looked back at him, her brows raised in disbelief. "You think we're being led around like a couple of ponies at a horse show?"

His heart rate move from a trot to a gallop. "Look at the evidence. Everything seems staged. It hit me this afternoon when I saw the knife sticking out of Otis Whittley. Your knife." He couldn't keep the tremble of excitement out of his voice. "Five years ago your family's name came up, but I've yet to arrest any one of them for anything. I moved to auto theft so I could keep tabs on them. You don't believe they were involved. Maybe they weren't."

He got up and slid onto the sofa. "I end up in the trunk of the very same car you're going to repo. It's almost like our meeting was prearranged. It sounds crazy, but some patterns are."

Shame moved through Kate's mind and gravitated into her body. It left her flushed and agitated. She had to tell him the secret. What would he do? How would he react? Her nerve flattened. The statute of limitations wasn't up.

"You think we're being manipulated?"

"Yeah. It makes sense. You're hired to repo cars. It looks legit. I'm the investigating officer."

She tried to soothe her frayed nerves. He was talking nutty, but what if he was on to something? "I was solicited for the repossession job. David Copeland called me out of the blue. I didn't know who he was, but I was broke, just trying to pay Jake's medical bills. He called when I was down to my last quarter."

"You see? This theory is solidifying. Things are starting to make sense. Callahan told me this afternoon that Whittley's Beamer was fitted with LoJack. Someone besides me had a bead on him. I had your car checked. If my hunch is right, Callahan will find it's been wired, too."

Mick tried to relax, but he couldn't. The knowledge pounded deep into his brain and anchored itself around his soul. They were game pieces. Joined together by a person or persons with a depraved mind. They'd killed in macabre fashion, and they'd kill again.

"We need to leave tonight. We're going underground."

Concern flashed across her face. He reached out to her. "It's not safe here…or anywhere. We have to assume they know where we are all the time."

"You're scaring me."

He took hold of her hand and pulled her against him. "I'm not telling you this to frighten you, I'm telling you because things could get hairy." Mick closed his eyes, trying to look ahead to the conclusion. What was the prize? What did the assailants have to gain? Why Kate?

The splinter of glass startled her. She bolted upright, but Mick pulled her onto the floor before she had time to process what was happening.

A fiery burn invaded her eyes and singed her sinuses, sending fire down her throat. She fought to breathe and closed her eyes, but the burn only intensified. "Mick!" she screamed, reassured when he grabbed her arm.

"It's tear gas."

"I've got to get out of here… I can't breathe." Pressure built inside of her chest, like a bucket of bricks pushed up against her.

"Come on." He pulled her to her feet. She steadied herself against him. Her senses in a tailspin, her knees buckled, but Mick's arm kept her from going down.

"Down the hall."

"Outside," she yelled, trying to open her eyes enough to see the front door. She pulled toward the door, but he pulled harder. She could just make out a canister lying below the window, spewing the toxic gas into the room.

"No, Kate." Mick grabbed the device and chucked it out the hole it had come in, scooped her into his arms and bolted down the hall.

She held on to him, feeling the power and determination in his body. Why weren't they running out of the house? She needed air. Fresh air.

Hugging him tighter, she let trust replace her desire to run.

Mick opened the door at the back of the hall, slipped inside and shut it. He put her down and yanked the bedspread off of the bed. Using it, he stuffed the fabric into the crack under the door. "Come in here." His eyes, nose and throat burned with the chemical agent, but he had to tend Kate and call 911. He pulled her into the bathroom and closed the door. "Strip."

"What!"

"It's the only way. The chemical is on your clothing and your skin. Undress. I'll run the shower." He turned on the water, adjusted it and tried to see through the wall of tears that poured from his eyes. Whoever had lobbed the tear gas through the window was waiting outside for them, but he wasn't going to risk Kate's life. "Get in, I'll dial 911."

He guided her to the shower stall and opened the door. Tears blurred his vision, but he could make out the rosy glow of her skin. The silhouette of her curvaceous body. Desire sparked deep inside of him. He wanted to smooth his hands over every inch of her, feel the swell of her breasts, elicit a response from deep in her soul. He closed the shower door behind her and shuffled out of the bathroom, feeling his way to the nightstand.

Pulling the phone from its cradle, he called 911.

"WHOEVER DID THIS is long gone, Mick."

Mick ran the end of the towel over his wet hair again and squared his shoulders to Callahan. "Figures. Did you find anything outside?"

"Couple of sets of footprints in the flower bed under the window. I'm having them cast right now. The canister might have some prints on it."

"We'll hope." Mick looked over at Kate. She sat on a kitchen stool, wrapped in his robe. The whites around her eyes were a deep shade of pink and she was still blinking back tears. It was a good thing they'd stayed inside. His suspicions were confirmed. Whoever had put the canister through the window did it so they could grab Kate when she fled the house.

Someone wanted her with a vengeance, but so did he.

"Anything on the car plate from this afternoon?"

"Stolen. Weeks ago."

Chapter Nine

"I don't think this is a good idea."

"Relax. It's going to work. Aim the light higher." Mick slid his fingertips along the trim around the door. "Aunt Bunny gave me her blessing and told me where to find the spare." He felt the key with his fingers and slid it off the narrow ledge.

"Maybe you're not comfortable with this plan. I have my doubts, too, but it's got to be done. The suspects are unpredictable and their attempts on you have escalated. If we can't draw them into a defensive position, we can't arrest them." Mick searched her upturned face in the glow of the flashlight beam. He needed her with him, a hundred-and-ten percent.

"I know you're right, but it's risky."

"Have some faith in me." He touched her cheek and she closed her eyes for a moment.

Desirous thoughts drummed in his mind as

she turned into his palm. Her skin was warm, soft, forbidden. "This will end soon, then you can pick up your son and go home."

She smiled at him, a slow seductive smile that sent his thoughts into hyperspace.

He swallowed his frustration and opened the screen door, slid the key into the lock and pushed it open. "I think this place was compliments of husband number four."

"The spoils of divorce?"

"No…old age, followed by death. Aunt Bunny always seems to marry the feeble ones." He stepped into the room and flipped the light switches to the living-room fixture and the porch light.

The smell of stale air inside the shut-up cottage was infused with the woodsy scent of the swamp. Slipcovers had been pulled over the living-room furniture and a fine layer of dust coated the end tables.

"She'd go into a dust-induced coma if she saw this place right now."

"You think?"

He turned toward Kate, who'd already moved into the kitchen and opened the cupboard below the sink.

"Neat freak, with an eccentric flair. I remember going to her house and sitting on a white sofa, afraid to move."

"Or breathe?"

"You had an aunt Bunny?"

"No. An aunt Joy."

She pulled out a can of furniture polish and a rag. "I'll dust the tables, you pull the slips."

"Deal." He followed her into the living room and pulled the fabric covers one by one, to expose overstuffed couches in a vivid shade of lime-green. "We'll be safe here. No one knows about this place." He heard the hiss of the furniture polish can and breathed in the scent of lemon that took over the air in the room. The sway of Kate's body as she rubbed the cleaner into the wood on the tabletops revved him up.

"You make it sound like these guys know us inside out." She finished the last table surface and turned to face him.

"They do, or they seem to." He fixed his gaze on her.

She shook her head back and forth in denial. "That's crazy. You don't expect me to believe that?"

"That's exactly what I expect. It's the only thing that's going to keep you alive. You can't let your guard down. Your car was fitted with LoJack." He moved close to her.

"Are you serious?"

"Callahan found a device. They're interested in your travel habits. You're the target."

"This can't be happening."

"If my hunch proves out, once we surface again they'll be pissed. I'd bet they do whatever it takes to assure it never happens again."

"What if you're wrong? What if they don't do anything to draw our attention. No warning shots, no waving arms or yelling, 'Hey you idiots we're over here.' Maybe they just decide it's time for me to die?"

"Whoa. I'm never going to let that happen." He put his arms around her and pulled her against his chest. A big mistake he decided as he inhaled her sultry scent and felt the womanly curves of her body pressed to his.

"How long are we going to hide?" She pulled away.

"Three days, four max. Just long enough for them to realize they've lost track of us."

"This is scary."

"Let it go for tonight." He took her hand. "We'll get you settled in. There's time to play Suzie homemaker tomorrow. I want you upstairs in the loft bedroom. Lock the door at the top of the landing. I'll take the couch."

He flicked the light switch at the bottom of

the stairs and followed her up to the wooden landing. Being so close to Kate was a mental exercise in restraint.

She opened the door and fiddled for the light switch. It flipped on with a decisive click. "It's a little sparse, but it'll work."

Wisps of cobwebs dangled from the pitched ceiling and moved gently in the air currents sent out by opening the door. A twin-size bed was pushed against one wall and a tiny nightstand with a candlestick lamp sat next to the bed. Scatter rugs in startling hues of pink dotted the hardwood floor.

"I'll get these. We can't have spider dreams keep you awake."

"Gee thanks." She watched him jump and swat the cobwebs, bringing them down one by one. The motion of his body stirred want inside of her and she tried to imagine what it would be like to be with him.

"I'll help you make the bed." His back was to her and she watched him pull sheets and blankets out of a cubby closet tucked underneath the eaves.

Focus. She redirected her erotic thoughts and pulled the dust cover off. Underneath a worn patchwork quilt covered the mattress.

"Aunt Bunny said this stuff was clean."

She pulled back the quilt and watched Mick scoop up the linens in his arms.

"Here, let me." She spotted a fitted corner. "I've got a sheet. Were there any pillows in there with the spiders?" Her hand brushed his in the pile of linens. The contact sent her heart rate up. She studied him, wondering if the brief touch had jolted him, too.

The detailed lines of his face were shadowed in the dim light coming from the fixture overhead, but there was no mistaking the wicked smile on his lips.

Desire, like liquid fire, coursed in her veins, but she held back. He hated her, didn't he? Hated her family? So why did she feel so willing to give herself to him…now…tonight?

Everything slowed to half speed when he tossed the bedding onto the mattress in one giant heave. His arms were around her before she could move. She breathed in his scent, a combination of clean skin and lime.

His essence invaded her mind and she raised her mouth to his. He kissed her, long…slow…deep. A lover's kiss. Laced with the promise of things to come. Satisfaction of a need drove her beyond her physical body and into a state of ecstasy.

Mind blank, her thoughts erased by the sensations that pulsed through her. She'd lost her perspective, lost her will to resist...lost her heart?

The kiss ended. It took her a moment to realize he'd pulled away. First his lips, then his body. She opened her eyes, plopped down on the end of the bed and took a deep breath.

He stared out the window, his hands on his hips. "I'm sorry, Kate." He turned to face her, the burn of desire smoldering in his eyes. "I'll be the first to say it. I'm out of line."

She managed to smile at him, and hung on to the warm afterglow enveloping her body. "It goes both ways. I'm not some innocent flower who's never been picked." She searched his face and tried to see beyond the decisive set of his jaw. Only the glimmer in his pale green eyes told the truth. He wanted her, too; he was a man on fire.

His arms dropped to his sides and he sat down next to her. "Tension. We're both venting. This is the first night in weeks we can relax. No one knows we're here, it's as good as a bottle of wine for cutting loose inhibitions."

"I've never had an inhibition feel like that."

"Me neither."

Their connection cemented, but didn't cure. Could she tell him about that night in May? Put herself on the line? He was sure to hate her more. Distrust her every word from now on. But the moment she found herself in was too perfect.

"Help me make the bed." She stood up.

"Sure." Mick pulled the sheet taunt and slipped it onto the corner of the mattress. They finished the task together and she walked him to the bedroom door.

"Lock it when I leave. Don't open it for anyone."

"Okay."

"Get some rest. Think of this as a vacation."

"I'll try."

Mick stepped onto the small landing outside the door and listened to her turn the lock. He was glad it was there to prevent him from going to her in the middle of the night. He wanted to be inside with her. Holding her body, stroking her skin. Damn the professional straitjacket. His badge. The rules.

She'd managed to drag his heart over the line in a game of tug-of-war. Could he drag it back to the right side? Did he want to?

Moving down the stairs, he tested the weight of his new reality. He hadn't felt this alive in a long time, but an emotional stake in Kate's life could make him careless. Take away his edge. Once his emotions were hooked up to the circuit, anything could happen. He'd have to guard against it, fight it anytime it surfaced.

The low-pitched moan of a board on the front porch stopped him at the bottom of the stairwell.

Someone was outside?

He turned the light off and poked his head out in time to catch a glimpse of a shadow as it stalled at the front door, outlined on the light curtain over the window.

Popping the snap on his shoulder holster, he slid his service revolver out of its cradle. Sweat formed on his forehead. His nerves twisted tight. The dead air in the room seemed to suffocate him as his heart rate cranked up and his lungs demanded more oxygen.

He was the only one between Kate and the front door, and he was already worried about her.

Shaking it off, he stepped into the hallway and stayed close to the wall. He'd made sure they weren't followed. Not even his supervisor knew exactly where they were.

Standing ready at the mouth of the hall, he watched the shadow pause at the door. He raised his gun and aligned the sight on the dark target.

Knuckles on wood broke his concentration.

"Knock. Knock. Bunny?" a male voice called out. "Are you home?"

Mick relaxed his stance, but didn't put his pistol away. Moving forward, he stopped at the front door and brushed the curtain aside.

An elderly gentleman stood outside on the front porch. "Hi. I'm Fred Picard, your next-door neighbor."

"Just a minute." Mick dropped the curtain, holstered his weapon and opened the door, but left the screen closed as a precaution.

"I saw the lights on over here and wondered who'd arrived. Bunny always calls us if she's coming to the cottage. We're part of a neighborhood watch program." He seemed to puff up a bit. "I like to check before I call the police."

He managed a friendly smile, but kept his caution. "Mick Jacoby, Bunny's nephew. I'm spending a couple of days here with my girlfriend. With Aunt Bunny's permission...of course."

"Come over from the city?"

"Yeah." He hated nosy people, but he was glad his aunt had a neighbor like Fred Picard.

"Well, welcome to our little place on the planet. Let me know if I can give you any assistance. There are some terrific places to eat in Slidell and there's a little grocery store, café, half a mile down the road."

"I appreciate that. There's not much here in the way of supplies."

Picard turned to leave. "I'll see if the missus has any extras and bring them over in the morning. That should hold you until you get to the grocery store."

"I appreciate that, Fred."

"Be talking to you in the a.m."

"By now." Mick watched him mosey down the porch steps and disappear into the darkness beyond the fringes of the porch light. He closed the door. So much for being incognito. He'd seen Picard types. By tomorrow afternoon there wouldn't be a single person along the stretch that didn't know Bunny's nephew from New Orleans was in town, and he had a girlfriend.

"Who was that?"

Mick spooked and looked up to see Kate coming down the hall toward him. She was a sexy vision in a flowing white nightgown that did little to conceal what was underneath. His blood heated in his veins. "A neighbor. Saw the lights and decided to investigate."

"You don't look happy about that."

"It's great if you're elderly and alone, but not if you're trying to hide out. I'd bet he has my aunt on the phone right now. Never mind that it's close to midnight."

"It'll be okay. I doubt he rolls in the same circle as our stalkers." She ran her hand down his forearm, sending shock waves into his body, but before he could reciprocate she turned and walked back down the hall. He listened to her hesitant steps up the stairs. Heard the door close, but not lock. The invitation had been telegraphed in her touch. It rocked him like an explosion tamped deep down in him.

He closed his eyes and fought the burn of insatiable need. It would be so easy to go to her. Easy to make love to her, but he couldn't let it happen. The minutes stretched as tight as his nerves until he heard the lock slide into place.

"Good night…Kate." He crashed onto the sofa to wait for dawn.

KATE AWOKE TO THE AROMA of fresh coffee and the smell of bacon. She rolled over and looked out the bedroom window. The sun was beginning to crest the tops of the cypress trees around the cottage. It had to be ten or later.

Slipping out of bed, she put on her robe. It was going to be tough to face Mick this morning, she decided as she finger combed her hair. She'd made an idiot of herself last night. The invasive thought of his body next to hers in the narrow bed had only kept her awake and added to her sexual frustration.

She couldn't let it happen again. Couldn't let

lust drive them into a situation they'd both regret. She headed downstairs expecting to see him at the kitchen table, but the kitchen was empty. A neat stack of blankets sat on one end of the sofa.

The smell of coffee pulled her into the kitchen and she poured a cup. The small cottage was quiet, peaceful. He must be outside. She pushed out of the screen door.

"Good morning, sunshine."

She started, jostling coffee everywhere. "Don't do that!"

He sat in an oversize rocking chair near the end of the porch, grinning at her, a pleased-with-himself smile that enhanced his good looks and made her knees weak. She increased her grip on the wet mug and moved toward the rocker he pulled in closer to his own.

"You snuck up on me last night. I had to return the favor."

"Very funny." She sat down next to him, feeling his heat even though a hint of breeze stirred the air.

"This is the life, don't you think?" He touched her hand for an instant.

She eyed the layout of the place now that daylight had arrived. "Near perfect, I'd say. The only thing missing is Cody. He'd enjoy throwing rocks in the pond and playing on the tire swing." She looked him over. "Don't tell me you're thinking retirement already?"

"No, but since you mentioned it, this would be a great place. You could bake cookies for the grandkids, I could pal around with the neighborhood geezer squad, enforce lights out at eleven. Teach them to nail a silhouette target in the center of mass with big guns. What could be better?"

Contentment had softened the hard edges of his face, giving her a rare glimpse into his soul. She resisted the need to touch him, to explore his heart. "If I didn't know better, I'd think you were serious."

"Who's to say I'm not. Don't you want those things in your life? Family, home…a husband." The question and his inquisitive stare bored into her.

Drawing a sip of coffee, she wished she could hide the flame of heat she felt in her cheeks. "Yes. Yes I do, but I haven't found the one I want to share it with."

"I did…once, but I let it slip away."

"You were a good father to Megan, a good husband to Natalie… I know it, I feel it."

He closed his eyes, then opened them again. They'd taken on a misty quality. "I could have done better. I could have protected them."

"No one knows what life will bring." She reached for his hand and they locked fingers. "We're here today, gone tomorrow and all we have in between are the little moments we can fill up with life, with love. It's not the big things we do, it's the energy we put into making special moments every day. That's what counts."

"How'd you become an expert?"

"Do you know a single kid who races to school to tell his friends his dad works fourteen-hour days so they can live in a nice house? What sticks is…my dad taught me to ride my bike. We made s'mores in the backyard over the barbecue and burned them to a crisp. That's what gets remembered…that's what counts. It's life, Mick. And love. Children just have a way of sharpening the point."

"Megan had those moments with me." He smiled and she felt his fingers relax.

Her heart flexed in her chest. She had to tell him. She didn't want her secret wedged between them. It would only hold them apart. "I have something to tell you."

"More life philosophy?" He leaned forward in his chair. "I'd like to get your take on second chances."

His eyes had taken on a sleepy half-lidded look that made her breath catch in her throat.

Her mouth went dry. She took a sip from her coffee cup and watched him over the rim. They'd come so far together. This confession could be their end.

"It's about that…night."

Mick's emotions dammed to a stop and bunched into knots. He swallowed hard as her words penetrated his brain. A confession?

He stared at her, watched her lick her lips and witnessed the flare of heat in her cheeks. His heart accelerated in his chest, racing like a freight train. He needed to hear her confess, but he also wanted to slam his fists against his ears to shut it out.

"I boosted a car that night, in your neighborhood. I'm the Robear you've been chasing."

Chapter Ten

Kate's words bit into him and shredded the shaky trust he'd given her. He released her hand and stood up. Air. He needed air. Where the hell was the air? He leaned onto the porch rail, his back to her, and squeezed his eyes shut.

"But I didn't hit them, Mick, as God is my witness, I didn't kill them. I'll tell you everything I know about that night. I promise. Just believe me. Please."

The chair creaked against the wooden deck. He anticipated her approach, but wasn't prepared when she touched his back with her hand. The gesture scorched him. He turned around, prepared to exact a price from her, but he stopped. Her hair had fallen over her face. Wet lines of tears squeezed from her eyes and dripped from her chin. She looked like a child standing before him and her anguish released his mercy.

"Kate." He brushed her hair behind her ears and pulled her into his arms. She was guilty of a felony. The statute of limitations hadn't run out. He could arrest her...maybe he should...but hadn't she just told him the very thing he wanted to hear? Where was the vindication he hungered for? That whisper of satisfaction down deep in his soul?

"Come on. Sit down." He moved her into the chair and knelt in front of her. "May 10, are you sure?"

"Yeah." She sucked in a huge breath and wiped her eyes. "I boosted a silver Mercedes a block over, it was around eleven. I thought I'd been had. There were lights and sirens everywhere, but I realized there must have been an accident because they never came for me. I drove to the shop where Dylan and Jake took the Mercedes apart."

His mind went numb. He'd seen the police report on the silver Mercedes and the timetable matched her account. Natalie and Megan were hit around eleven and the car was stolen in that time frame.

"Are you sure? Will you swear one of your brothers wasn't boosting that night?"

"It was me. I'm the one you want."

Relief surged in his mind and he pulled her against him.

"I should have told you sooner, but the admission could put me away. I have Cody to take care of, but it makes you right about me. I'll take whatever decision you make."

"Three days Kate. We're here for three more days. By the time we get back to New Orleans the statute of limitations will almost be up." He held her. Felt her body tremble as she warred with her emotions. He'd had his trust smashed and restored in a couple of minutes. But what about her family? Could he trust their word, too?

"This is heavy stuff."

She retreated and smoothed her tears. "You won't regret this. I promise." Her expression was soft, innocent, inviting.

His resistance crumbled like mud brick and he lowered his mouth to hers, tasting her sweet coffee kiss with his tongue, soaking her into his soul.

WHERE THE HELL WERE THEY? He bit down hard on the butt of the cigar clamped tight between his teeth and brought his night-vision binoculars to his eyes.

Kate's house was dark, too, just like Jacoby's. He hadn't expected there would be anyone there, but maybe Mick would screw up and allow her to come home for a night. Her Bronco was parked in the driveway where it had been for days, but he'd have known if it had moved.

"Dammit." Jacoby had taken them on the road. It would be harder to track them. Frustration sizzled and exploded inside of him. Mick would pay for this. He'd wait the stupid bastard out, but he wouldn't let it happen again.

He'd crawl inside Mick's mind and camp out. Anticipate his next move before he made it. Tossing the equipment onto the seat, he fired up the car engine. Rigging Jacoby's unit with Lo-Jack could have saved him some sleep.

Anger simmered in his mind. They had to come back, and when they did, he'd be waiting….

MICK NOSED INTO a parking spot at the side of the police station and shut off the engine. Kate hadn't said two words to him since they'd left the protection of the cottage and her mood seemed to match the gray of the storm clouds overhead. "You owe me a set of elimination prints. Care to accompany me inside to central booking?"

"I'd rather walk over to Jackson Square and get a coffee."

He resisted the urge to touch her, then succumbed and brushed her cheek with his hand. "I can't let you do that."

"What are you worried about?" She looked at him, the glitter of challenge in her dark eyes barely concealed before she dropped her gaze. "I'm MacGyver, remember? You said so yourself."

That was before he'd kissed her. Before he'd seen her vulnerable nature, her tender heart. "I do remember. But we're not in the clear, not until I nail these creeps."

"I need to breathe. I want to feel normal again. Please." Desperation shadowed her face and she gave him a half smile that depleted his resignation.

"Let's go upstairs. I think I have a solution."

They climbed out of the car and strolled to the rear entrance of the station. Mick punched in the security code and listened for the door lock to accept the numbers. He didn't often use the back door and he hoped he'd remembered them correctly. They hadn't been changed in eons. "How do you feel about police uniforms?"

"Not much of a fashion statement. Serviceable, but they look horrible on the runway."

That was the Kate he wanted. The one he liked to be around. The door accepted the code and buzzed open. He turned the knob and followed her into the building. "The service elevator is over here. I use it whenever I don't want to be spotted until I'm ready, but I can't beat that damn security camera." He gestured to the eye on the wall above the door.

"You? I'd never have taken you for an introvert."

"I'm not. But when Schneider wants my reports on his desk and they're not finished…"

The elevator dinged and the doors slid open. "There are a couple of uniforms in the break room with curves in the right places. I think one of them might fit you. With a vest on underneath and an armed escort…I'll feel okay with you out in the real world."

"You can't be serious?"

"I am." The elevator glided to a stop and the doors opened.

"If that's what it takes to get a minute's worth of normal, I'll do it."

He led her along a narrow hallway. "My office is here and this is the break room."

"All the comforts of home?"

"Almost." He pulled open the door to a small closet. "These have been in here for so long, I don't remember who they belong to. This one looks good." He held it out for her to take. "You can put it on in the ladies' room down the hall. I'll get you a vest and send it up with a female officer."

"Mick?" He looked into her glowing brown

eyes and saw a flash of gratefulness. "I'll be all right. I'll keep my head down, my senses on full alert."

"I know you will." He looked away and tried to shake the tension that bound up between his shoulder blades. He'd have to be satisfied she would be safe without him hovering over her like a prison guard. "I'll get that vest. Officer Nelson can show you how to put it on. I'll see you downstairs."

"Are you sure this is legal? Won't I be impersonating an officer in this getup?"

"Probably." He left her with a perplexed smile on her pouty lips and a sense of satisfaction in his mind. She was a long way from where she'd been five years ago, stealing cars, living life on the edge, to being decked out in blue.

He stalked into the patrol room and spotted Officer Tina Nelson, sipping coffee from a bright red cup.

She saw him and smiled. "Well…will you look what snuck in the back door."

"You been hanging out in the tape room again, Tina?"

"Yeah, so I can stare at that gorgeous mug of yours?"

"Your mug isn't so bad."

"I'll take that as a compliment, coming from

you, but you're only here because your ears are on fire. Schneider thinks you went AWOL four days ago and he let everyone know."

"I did. Had some vacation time coming. Decided I'd get out of this hole. No secret there."

"It is if you vacationed with a material witness." She winked at him and raised her cup again, polished it off and set it down on the counter.

"Who fed you that line of bull?" Mick shoved his hands into his pockets and tried to relax.

"Just tread easy on Schneider. He's grouchy today."

"Thanks, I'll keep that in mind. I've got a favor to ask."

"Ask away."

"That material witness is upstairs in the ladies' room with a uniform on. Do you think you can loan her your extra vest and show her how to put it on?"

Tina wrinkled her nose. "Sure. Always a bridesmaid, never a bride."

Mick shook his head. "Your turn will come."

"Promises, promises." She brushed past him, smiling as she left the room.

Officer Tina Nelson had always been a temptress and he enjoyed returning her suggestive banter, but it lacked its edge today.

"Hey, Jacoby." Ryan Tassano entered the patrol room. "Schneider's gunning for you. He didn't look too happy when he found out you were in the building."

"As long as his face isn't red, I'm safe. Don't you have the foot patrol down in Jackson Square?"

"Yeah. I'm just in for a briefing on some purse snatchers. I should be back out there in ten."

"Would you escort my material witness?"

Ryan checked his watch. "Sure. If you give me five minutes, I'll meet you at the desk. Anything I should know?"

He considered the officer's question. He couldn't tell him how dangerous Kate Robear really was to his state of mind. "Don't let her out of your sight. A couple of thugs are stalking her and they mean business. She wants to go over to Café du Monde. She's not a prisoner. She can do it with or without my approval. Just so you know, she's wearing a uniform. Together you'll look like a couple of beat cops on the job."

"No problem. What kind of timetable are we…"

Following Ryan's line of sight at the point his words had trailed off, he found Kate outlined in the doorway of the patrol room.

"Snap out of it, Ryan. You have a fetish for women in blue?"

"No. But that's about the best blue I've seen in a while."

Mick let his stare linger on her longer than he should have and closed his mouth the moment he realized it hung open.

"I don't," Ryan said, turning to him, eyebrows raised, "but you do."

Mick glared at him and wished he could wipe the knowing smile off Ryan's face without violence. "Just take care of her. I'm going down to smooth things over with Schneider. Half an hour, forty-five minutes. If you aren't back, I'll come looking."

"Don't I know it," Ryan said. "I'd come looking, too."

Mick brushed past her and pulled in a whiff of her sultry scent, heavy on exotic floral. "Nice outfit, Miss Robear."

"Thank you, Officer." She smiled at him as he slipped into the elevator and turned to face her. She was a beautiful woman. Strong, sexy, approachable. The doors slid shut and he relaxed against the wall. He was screwed. In over his head. Drowning.

The elevator stopped and he stepped out, resisting the urge to tiptoe past the front desk. He ducked into Schneider's office and closed the door behind him.

His boss had just raised a coffee cup to his mouth when he spotted Mick over the rim and grinned. "Here for your lashing?"

"Something like that. You did a heck of a job convincing everyone I'd flaked out with my witness in tow."

"You like that, huh? Nothing like a pissed-off supervisor with a big mouth to get things stirred up. Now, you want to tell me why you wanted the information tossed around like beads at Mardi Gras?"

Mick pulled a stick of gum out of his shirt pocket and folded it into his mouth. "Kate Robear. Repossession agent."

"Your material witness?"

"That and a lot more. She led me to a chopper with some information."

Surprise crossed Schneider's face and disappeared into his laugh lines. "What ya got, Mick?"

"Smuggling, but that's not the worst of it. Rumor on the street is there's a cop involved. If he's in this department, I wanted to be sure he knew we'd disappeared."

"You're not making sense."

"Callahan found a tracking device on her car and there was one on Otis's BMW. I hope the suspects will make a move to install LoJack on my unit. Maybe we'll get them this time." Mick let out a breath, desperate to put it together. "I think she's been repossessing cars loaded with something. What, I don't know. But I believe Otis, Romaro and Durant were all in on the same action. Kate's list of repo jobs ties them all together. Somewhere things went sour."

Schneider cleared his throat and rocked back in his chair. "Durant was caught with a load of cash. What if that's our contraband? Our cop is taking a cut and offering them protection in return."

"Makes sense. Maybe Otis and Romaro tried to slip out with the green and our guy killed them, but Durant got away?" Mick rolled the scenario in his mind. "It still doesn't explain why he's after Kate."

"Have you picked her brain for information, connections, anything?"

"Yeah."

"Is it possible she beat our suspects to the money in the BMW, and now they want it back? It's motive, Mick."

"Her only contact is with a middleman, David Copeland, cell phone only, no face-to-face."

"I'll subpoena everyone's phone records, see if we can locate him, get an address."

"Besides, I've been with her from the moment she took the Beamer."

"This whole thing stinks like a federal case. The FBI can't be too far behind the smell. I've got a buddy in the bureau. I'll give him a call."

"Whoa, Ben. I want my witness protected. This is all speculation. We need some solid evidence before we bring them in and if it's drug money, every law enforcement agency with an acronym is coming to the party."

"Then you better get on it." Schneider shot him a smile. "Just make sure you keep Ms. Robear safe."

"I'm doing my best. We're moving 24/7."

"Good, keep it that way."

Mick sat back in his chair. "Is Whittley's autopsy in?"

"Came in yesterday. Died from a stab wound directly to the heart, but there were additional stab wounds on the body. All shallow, non-lethal."

"Torture?"

"Looks that way."

"What about the butcher knife?"

"The M.E. says it was done after the fatal wound was inflicted."

"Someone wanted something from him pretty bad. Maybe a stack of money?"

"That would be my guess." Ben picked up his

coffee mug and took a swallow. "If the money thing plays out, where is it?"

"Spent, stashed. Who knows, but I can save you some time on the knife in Otis's chest. It was stolen from Kate Robear's house a couple of months ago. You'll find it listed on the break-in report along with some missing personal items. I'll vouch for her. She never had time to kill him, or hammer the knife in."

"Figures, but there might be some hope for finding out who did. We got good news this morning off the fax machine. Orlando Durant is heading our way. He fought extradition and lost. He claims he has information about Otis and Romaro. He wants protection."

"That would mean he knows the kind of suffering Whittley and Romaro's killer can inflict, but does he know who the killer is?" Mick shifted in his chair, uncomfortable with the knowledge that these guys wanted Kate.

"I won't know until I question him, but maybe we can get something from another source. Otis has an elderly mother. Mary Bell Whittley. She's been notified of his death, but she was too upset to be questioned about his activities. She's in Spring Hill Retirement Home." Schneider pulled out a notepad and scribbled down the address. "I don't suppose you'd like to handle that?"

"Love to." He stood up and took the paper. "We've got something serious on our hands."

Schneider nodded. "Tough part is you never know who will get pulled in."

"I'll keep you informed."

"See that you do."

KATE PICKED UP the small coffee cup and wished it was a large mug the moment the strong coffee touched her tongue and flowed down her throat. She missed normal. Over the rim of the cup she eyed Officer Tassano. He was cute, but too boyish around the ears, she decided when she found herself comparing him to Mick. Her heart rate shot up, but she related it to the jolt of caffeine she'd just swallowed. Still, she couldn't keep him off her mind.

Staring out toward the Mississippi, she tried unsuccessfully to stop the images, and focused on the officer as a distraction. "How long have you been with the police department?"

An ear-splitting boom shattered her question and she dove for cover under the table.

"What the hell!" Officer Tassano bolted to his feet as another explosion shook the square and rattled the dishes above her head.

She stood up and stared in the direction the explosions had come from.

Reality was beginning to sink into the crowd. Like hundreds of frightened animals, people absorbed the panic.

She could see it in the twisted looks on their faces. Everyone skittered for cover.

Boom! Another explosion rang out in Jackson Square.

"Come on. Let's get back to the station." Officer Tassano began to work through the unstable crowd outside of the open café.

Kate struggled to keep up with him. Fear worked in her stomach and split her nerves as the roar of the crowd grew to a crescendo and the panicked mass turned into a stampeding mob.

She tried to spot the officer, but she was being bumped and pulled along in the throng of people. *Mick.* The need for his protection came alive inside of her as she pushed against the crowd, trying desperately to work her way across the square.

Focused on the spires of St. Louis Cathedral, she fought against the infectious panic that skittered through her body. Mick would come, he would find her, if only she could get close to him.

The feel of a large hand on her wrist gave her an instant of relief, but it was followed by horror when she looked up into the face of a man she didn't know.

"Let go!" She jerked hard, but he held her fast, pulled her into the bushes and forced her to the ground.

His eyes were wild, his movements jerky, like an addict in need of a fix.

"Shut up!" he bellowed, looking around.

The protest died on the end of her tongue. The gleam of a knife blade protruded from his fist. She looked for a way out, but they were tucked behind a bank of shrubs. Lost in a foliage jungle, while the world went crazy outside.

Mick would never find her in time. Terror burned inside of her and she stared at the man in front of her, at the knife he moved so close to her throat she could almost feel it bite into her flesh.

"Where is it, bitch? Where's the money you took from the car?"

THE SLAP OF SCHNEIDER'S office door against its stop brought Mick's head around. Benjamin Schneider was a big man and Mick felt the floor beneath his feet tremble as Ben rushed out of his office and stalled at the front desk.

"Get SWAT and every available officer down to Jackson Square. All hell broke loose."

Mick whirled around. Kate was down there. "What's going on?"

"Someone set off a load of smoke grenades. The whole place looks like a war zone."

Images of Kate spun in his head. His legs felt supercharged as he raced out of the main doors at a full run, headed for the Square, via Royal Street.

He bolted around the corner at Pirates Alley, and slammed into a wall of people charging away from the scene, their faces pinched with panic. Swept along in their midst, he was being pulled farther and farther from Kate.

Mick lunged for a lamppost, wrapped his arms around the solid upright and climbed onto the concrete base. From his vantage point he scanned the crowd, desperation squeezing his insides.

The entire square was umbrellaed in a blanket of thick white smoke. People sat where they'd fallen in the ensuing panic. The SWAT team moved deliberately around the square, sweeping the area.

Most of the smoke canisters no longer spewed. Only a couple continued to emit puffs of smoke.

He looked into the sea of people behind him and hoped for a glimpse of Kate, but she wasn't there. Worry twisted in his stomach. If anything happened to her…

"Money. I don't have any money."

"You're lying. I'm going to cut you." For an instant he hesitated.

Run. She scrambled to her feet, but he pulled her down hard and straddled her.

She closed her eyes, the blade of the knife sticky against her sweat-slicked throat.

For an instant the smoke parted and Mick saw the bob of a head behind a bank of hedges. His breath caught on the edge of his heart. He bailed off the lamppost and sprinted toward her, surprised by the amount of relief that invaded his body, but there was caution, too, and he pulled his gun as he approached the thicket.

Mick dropped below the top of the hedge and glanced down the row. Caution and worry rolled inside of him and his heart jumped in his chest. He pulled back. A man straddled Kate. A knife to her throat. One wrong move and she'd be dead.

Chapter Eleven

Mick crawled to the opposite side of the row and stood up, gun raised. Shoot to kill plastered his heart and his mind.

"Drop the knife, or I'll blow you away." He stalked toward the man who held Kate. He watched a second of indecision flash across the man's grizzled features and prepared to double tap him.

"Toss it."

The assailant pitched the knife away and stood up.

Mick was on him in two seconds, but he stared down at Kate, who'd come to a sitting position. "Are you okay?"

She looked up at him and his heart melted into his shoes. She nodded.

Officer Tassano rounded the corner at a jog. "Man, I'm sorry. I lost her in the crowd."

"Get this scum out of here. I'm right behind you."

"No problem."

Mick listened to Tassano's cuffs ratchet tight. "Charge him with assault for starters."

"You got it." He dragged the man away.

Mick collapsed on the ground next to her and pulled her into his arms. No words passed between them; no words had to. He held her close, inhaling the scent of her hair as he pulled blades of dry grass out of it. His heart expanded in his chest and filled with emotion. Emotion he was afraid to put a name to. Emotion he wasn't sure he could suppress.

"I'm sorry. I should have been with you."

"He wanted to know where the money was."

"Money?" His gaze settled on her lips.

"He seems to think I have Otis's money."

It was useless to resist and he brushed a piece of leaf off her cheek. The motion and the touch sent a shock wave into him and he locked his gaze with hers. A slow smile spread over her lips and his resistance died. He dropped his head and covered her mouth with his. The contact satisfied the river of raw emotion that roared through him, but the result was a need for more.

He pulled back and focused on the misty

quality in her eyes, the wisps of her hair against her cheek, the tilt of her head to one side, like a girl with questions...or the answers. He wasn't sure.

"One stalker down, one to go." He took her hand and helped her to her feet. They waded into the crowd that had become more reasonable now that the excitement had died down.

"Did he hurt you?"

"No, but he threatened to."

"You're sure you're okay?"

"I'm fine."

"What happened?" Anger ate through his moment of euphoria and left him hungry for answers to why he felt as if he'd almost lost her."

"We were in Café du Monde, three or four explosions went off. Everyone got whipped into a panic and ran off. I tried to get away, but the crowd was too strong. I got separated from Officer Tassano."

He could only shake his head. Relief pulsed through him, taking his tension with it. "Come on, I'll take you up to my office so you can get changed before they call you to direct traffic."

Kate followed him into the building and onto the elevator, enduring a blast of heat when the doors slid open on the third floor. "Poor boy, hanging on the top floor."

"Something like that. I've got an AC in my window. I'd better turn it on."

"You haven't always been up here, have you?" She watched him slip a key into the door and open it. He stepped aside for her to enter.

"No."

"Want to tell me why you prefer heat to cool?" She knew she was probing. His office was about as far as you could get from homicide.

He motioned to a chair, smack against the wall and covered with files. "Let me." Scooping them up, he plopped them onto the desk.

She sat down and tried to imagine him in this little room, putting the heat to every chop shop in New Orleans. It smelled like him. Clean with a twist of lime. Various awards were neatly framed and hung on a white wall. Honors for a man who deserved one more award for saving her life. The desk he'd taken a seat behind was small and behind it he looked tough, gorgeous... alone.

"I'd had enough."

"Shell shock?" She focused her attention on him.

"That's one way to put it. When you've seen what I've seen a hundred times over, it changes you. Before you know it, you've lost your perspective."

"Is that why you took up hunting Robears?"

He leaned back in his chair and narrowed his eyes, as if the answer was there, but he didn't want to share it. She wanted to test him, to slip under his skin and shake him up. She needed to know if he reacted to her because she was a Robear or because she was a woman.

"Initially, yes. When the name surfaced, I wanted to hunt them down, but I've never been able to connect the dots. Five years, no arrests."

"What more proof do you need? The rumor, although true in part, was put up as a screen to hide the real killer."

Mick cocked his head and considered the new degree of spin she'd put on his quest. He'd been so sure the Robears were involved, he never considered anyone else.

"You're an amazing woman." She smiled at him and he saw a brief spark of surprise in her eyes. Amazing and dangerous.

"Let's get downstairs, I want to talk to Schneider, get his take on the smoke in the square and see if your assailant had anything to say."

She stood up, her eyes locked on his desk. He followed her line of vision and glanced at the file on the top of the stack, FRANK ROBEAR.

"Don't get me wrong, Kate." He grabbed the folder and put it on the bottom of the pile. "I'm just doing my job at this point. And you know he's not squeaky clean."

It was the look of injury in her eyes that nudged his heart. A look of trust betrayed. She was halfway out the door before he caught up with her and turned her around.

"Don't. Don't ask me to look the other way. It doesn't mean I'm right. It means I'm doing my job."

She wouldn't look at him, instead she chose to stare at the floor and bounce the toe of her shoe against it. "Yeah. Your job." Suddenly she looked up and he saw realization cross her face and furrow her forehead.

"I'm just a witness to you. Someone you plan to ditch after you've used me to tidy up your facts. If I hadn't had a couple of stalkers after me, I'd probably be in a cell somewhere. That's what you want. Right? Any Robear will do?"

"No…but I think you're holding out on me." He'd said it. Handed over the last piece of doubt stuck in his mind. Would she take it, or shove it back in his face?

She sagged against the wall as if a ten-ton rock hung around her neck. "I've told you everything of any value. There isn't any more."

"I want to believe you."

"Then do it. Use that thing between your ears and give me a break. Let me help you."

Mick pulled her toward the ladies' room, his anger beginning to boil. "Change." He watched her go inside and hung his head. She wanted him to accept her help? A Robear's help? First he'd have to admit he needed her digging around for information. His level of trust would have to take a high jump.

She stepped out of the ladies' room and took hesitant steps toward him. He felt like a jerk for not believing her and his anger cooled.

"Truce?"

"Since we're stuck with each other for now, I guess."

"Let's go." He followed her into the elevator and out onto the first floor. Mick focused on Schneider's office and leaned against the door frame. "Anything on the square?"

"Remote devices, not an amateur job. The bomb squad is analyzing them now."

"How many?"

"Five. Set off from outside the perimeter."

"Kate's assailant?"

"He lawyered up, but not before he denied having anything to do with Otis's murder. He claims Otis had something on David Copeland."

"Kate's boss?" Mick digested the information and wondered how Kate was involved. "Thanks, Ben. I'll talk to you tomorrow." He escorted Kate to central booking, mentally working the David Copeland angle.

"Hey, Bennett."

A clean-shaven officer looked up from behind his computer screen and nodded. "What ya got?"

"I need a set of elimination prints from this young lady. Keep them in-house and have a hard copy sent up to me."

"No problem." He stood up and came to the counter. "Ever been fingerprinted miss?"

"No." A wave of apprehension swelled inside her. "Will it take long?"

"No. The procedure is simple. I'll roll your fingers over a scanner."

She watched him rub a cloth over a small plastic pad and flip a button on the side of the unit. Bright light glowed from inside. He picked up a pen and a card from under the counter.

"Your full name?"

"Katherine Elizabeth Robear."

"Date of birth?"

"June 20, 1977."

"That'll do it. Please step around the counter."

Mick had taken a seat and seemed disinterested in the whole process. He'd probably witnessed it a thousand times.

"Let's get started."

"Okay." She floated through the process and was glad when he turned the machine off.

"You're done."

"Great."

He grinned at her and turned his attention to Mick. "I'll get these prints into the computer and a hard copy to you, ASAP."

Mick stood up and stretched, moving toward her in slow sexy strides. Her heart jumped, but he didn't say a word until they'd left through the front door of the station and stepped out into the heat of the afternoon.

"Want to finish your beignet over at Café du Monde?"

"Maybe another time. I think I swallowed it whole in all the commotion. It's stuck right about here." She indicated a spot on her chest, but he wasn't paying attention. Instead he'd taken a rigid stance on the top step of the stairs. She focused on the set of his shoulders, the way he scanned the street in front of them.

"We need to scout out our next overnight. Any particular end of town you'd like to try?"

"Home."

"Not an option." He moved her forward with his hand on the small of her back. Tension built in his neck and tightened his shoulders as he looked across the street, then up and down the sidewalk. People were moving again, not in a panic, but at a leisurely pace.

He couldn't explain his apprehension, the slow foreboding that climbed out of his gut and sneaked up his spine. But it was there. "Let's hurry it up."

"Sure." She tossed him a what's-going-on glance.

They hit the sidewalk and blended into the crowd, then broke loose and walked to the side of the station.

Mick opened the car door and closed it behind her, circled and took his place behind the wheel. His tension had eased by the time he put the key in and started the car.

"What was that about?"

Shifting into reverse, he glanced at her and saw worry lines around her mouth. "Don't know, don't even know if you'd understand."

"Try me."

He braked, put the car in drive and eased into the narrow street. "Have you ever felt like you were being watched? You can't put a name to that sixth sense, you just know it."

"Yes. I've felt it." She shifted in her seat. "That night, in the swamp, repossessing Otis's car, I had it then. That's when I smelled cigar smoke. They were there. Watching. Waiting to grab the car and kill the poor guy, but I got to it first."

"Probably. Judging from the evidence we collected, someone was there."

"They think I have Otis's money. They want it so bad they're willing to go through you." The color drained from her face, leaving her pale.

"Jackson Square was a distraction so they could take you, but it didn't work." He touched her hand where it lay in her lap and was rewarded with an emotional charge. "I won't let them get close to you again. The next one will have to come through a hail of bullets." He made eye contact with her, hoping he'd convinced her he was capable of taking care of her, but apprehension marred her face. Gently he raised his hand and stroked his thumb against her skin. She closed her eyes and took a deep breath.

"We'll get him, Kate. We have his buddy."

HE WATCHED THEM pull out and creep down the street from his vantage point.

Now he could relax. Anytime he wanted Kate, he could have her. From now on he'd be in control. No more escapes to secret locations beyond his reach. With some harmless smoke grenades as a distraction he'd made sure he could find them anytime.

Crawling inside Mick's head had been easy. He wasn't a very good cop.

A laugh brewed in his throat. He nipped the end off his cigar and shoved it into his mouth, flicked the lighter and puffed the smoke to life.

SPRING HILLS was pretty springy, Mick decided when the ornate wrought iron gate opened and an attendant approached.

"Your name, sir?"

"Jacoby, New Orleans Police Department. I'm here to speak with Mary Bell Whittley." He flashed his badge.

The attendant looked at his clipboard. "She's in the Magnolia complex. Through the gate and take a right. The parking lot is the first on the left."

"Thanks." Mick eased down on the gas pedal and followed the sweep of the cobble drive lined with magnolia trees. "I wonder what a place like this costs?"

"I pay three grand a month for Jake's care and that's bare bones. This has got to be more."

He had to agree. Someone was paying big bucks. His guess was it had been Otis. What would happen now that Otis was dead? Who would pay for his mother's care?

The cobble drive widened and opened up at the top of a small knoll. Nestled among a grove of oak trees was a complex fit for a king. "Send me here when I'm old." Mick chanced a glance at her.

"In your dreams, Mr. Jacoby. Besides Aunt Bunny's cottage fits you."

"Homey beats the heck out of champagne and caviar." Mick drove the car down a shallow decline, past a kidney-shaped swimming pool and a rose garden, where gray-haired ladies in large-brimmed hats tended to rose bushes and various other flowers. He was struck by the country club atmosphere.

A large plaque with MAGNOLIA in bright gold letters designated the parking lot. He nosed his unit in between two Cadillacs and killed the engine. "I'm speculating, but let's say Otis was covering the cost of his mother's care. Guessing it at six to ten grand a month, he's into this place sixty to a hundred-twenty thousand a year. You saw his shack, where does someone like Otis Whittley get money like that?"

"You mean *did* he get money like that? You can make it taking down cars, but you'd have to grab a couple a night, higher odds of getting caught. He was into something lucrative. Smuggling? Dealing drugs?"

"He's got no record. My case is based on him boosting the mayor's car. There was an eyewitness who named him. I could never get a handle on the guy. He was good, always looked over his shoulder, afraid of his shadow."

"He had good reason, didn't he?"

Glancing sideways, he looked at her. "He was running scared. The poor bastard probably didn't even know I was on to him, because he had a bigger problem. Let's go see if his mother knew what he was up to." Mick opened the car door.

The outside of Spring Hills was posh. Tall wooden doors carved with flowers barred the entrance of the stone building. A bell with a gold-lettered sign above it read PLEASE RING IN.

Mick pushed the button and heard the dainty chime of the bell echo inside the fortress. A small square in the middle of the door opened up.

"Can I help you?" a female voice questioned from inside.

Is this the Emerald City? Mick dismissed the stupid thought. The precaution was probably as much to keep the residents in as to keep the public out, but it still amused him.

"I'm Officer Jacoby, this is Kate Robear. We're here to see Mary Bell Whittley. Do you need to see my badge?"

"No. Matthew the gate attendant said you

would be arriving." With that the square in the door closed into itself and blended seamlessly into the wood carving.

"Wait, I'm Dorothy. I'm here to see the wizard."

"What?" Kate laughed and popped him with the back of her hand, just as the door opened. They both turned to find a young woman staring at them.

Her uniform consisted of a black skirt and a white blouse. She was pressed and prim all the way from her black shoes to the frown on her face. "Come in. Mary Bell is in the sitting room at the moment. She's been quite upset since her son's death. Follow me." She turned and strode away.

Mick could certainly understand how upset she was. He'd take it easy.

The floor was covered with thick carpet in a rich shade of burgundy. Raised wood panels lined the lower half of the hallway and wainscot divided it from the artwork spaced at even intervals along the wall. The hall emptied into a large room where small conversation areas had been formed with floral couches. A bank of bookshelves lined the far wall and in the north corner was a big-screen TV.

The room was empty except for a woman in a wheelchair. She had her back to them and stared out the window at the expanse of lush green lawn and a fountain.

"Mrs. Whittley? You have guests." The young woman touched her on the shoulder. The contact caused the woman to start.

"Oh dear girl, you frightened me."

"I am sorry." She turned the wheelchair to face Mick and Kate and politely excused herself.

"Mrs. Whittley, I'm Officer Jacoby, New Orleans Police Department, and this is Kate Robear." Mick shifted his weight, and a zing of sympathy shot through him.

The elderly woman's face was drawn, tired. Her eyes were swollen, no doubt from the tears she'd cried for her son. Even bad people have mothers who love them.

Mick sucked that knowledge in and used it to temper his attitude. "We're sorry for your loss."

The condolence turned her tear faucet on and she dabbed at her eyes with a dainty pink handkerchief. "Thank you, but I'm sure you're here for another reason. I wondered when you would come. Sit down, young man. Would you like something to drink?"

"No, thank you." Mick chanced a glance at Kate. She was perched on the edge of a deep sofa, trying not to fall in. An amused smile turned the corners of her mouth and she shot him a "here I go" look, then shoved back onto the couch.

He looked away to avoid the stir of humor she'd raised. This was not the time. Still she looked very small, immersed in the fluff of the sofa.

"Can I see your badge?"

"Sure." Mick pulled his badge off his belt and handed it to her.

She held it very close to her face, narrowed her eyes and squinted. Finally she tapped it with her fingernail and held it close to her ear. "Real. Good. You just can't be too careful these days." She handed it back to him.

"What do you mean, Mrs. Whittley?"

"There was a man here in early April, claimed to be a policeman. I talked to him in the dining room, but not before I checked his badge, just like that. The damn thing was tin. I told him to get himself right out the door. He got up and left."

"What did he look like?" Mick's curiosity flared. Otis was still alive when the cop had visited her.

"I've got cataracts, son. It's hard to see detail. I did look him up and down. He's a tall one, don't know what color his hair or eyes were.

Dressed in dark clothes head to toe and he smelled like the inside of a cigar box."

Mick saw Kate jolt forward on the couch. "Smoker, huh?"

"I'd say so."

"What kind of questions did he ask?"

"Before or after I thumped his badge?"

"Both."

"He wanted to know if I'd seen Otis lately, if he'd given me anything to hold for safekeeping. Then I asked him if I could see his badge. He got a little huffy with me, gave me some spiel about getting no respect...la-ti-da...then he handed it to me and I did just like I did to yours. It wasn't real. That's when I told him to leave. He was plenty upset, but he left."

"You did the right thing. When did you last see Otis?" Mick asked.

"The end of March. He dropped by for my birthday party. Didn't have much to say, but he seemed out of sorts."

"How so?"

"Jumpy. Nervous. Kept looking around, finally left before I even got my cake cut up, but he gave me these." She reached in at the collar of her blouse and pulled up a key tied on a long piece of purple yarn, then reached into her sweater pocket and pulled out a folded piece of paper. "It was Otis, God rest his soul, who told me not to trust anyone just because they claimed to be a policeman."

Her hand trembled as she held the paper and key out to Mick.

"Thank you. This could help us find out who... killed him."

She nodded. "I'll hold you to it, Officer. He was a good boy, just a little misguided. When he started to associate with questionable people, I tried to rein him in, but he was beyond my control and my health was shot."

Mick reached out and patted Mary Bell's hand. "I'm sure you did the best you could. Any chance you remember the names of those questionable people?"

"Clear as a bell. Alan Delancy. He's the one I figure pulled Otis in. Neighborhood boy down the street. They went to high school together. He always had an expensive car in the driveway. My Otis liked expensive cars."

Mick scribbled down the name. "How old would you guess Delancy is?"

"He and Otis were a couple of years apart, I'd say twenty-five, twenty-six."

"Do you have any idea what this key might go to, Mary Bell?"

"No, and I don't want to know. I didn't want

to risk it. I wasn't sure why he wanted me to keep that stuff. I'm no fool. I knew my Otis was into something bad, I didn't know if my heart could take it, so I put it away. He told me if anything happened to him, I was to give it to a real policeman."

"Can I read this note to you now?"

"I suppose…it can't hurt. He's gone."

Mick unfolded the slip of paper and read it out loud. "Sixty-seven, thirty-five, Makin. Does that mean anything?"

She pondered the information, tilted her head to the side, then straightened in her seat. Surprise crossed her face and melted into irritation. "That boy. I don't know how many times I asked him to keep my age quiet. I'm sixty-seven, my maiden name was Makin, and I grew up at thirty-five Chelmette Road out in Pennybrook. My youngest brother, Phillip, still has a little winter place out there at the homestead."

"Did Otis have access to the property?"

"I suppose so. There's a small house and a couple of outbuildings. Nothing worth stealing, so my brother didn't take any security measures."

"How long since he visited the place?"

"Years. Ten maybe."

A surge of excitement pumped through him.

"Thank you. You've been a great help. If you think of anything, give me a call. My number's on this card." Mick pulled a business card out of his wallet and pressed it into her hand.

She promptly put it to her face and focused, then unfocused. "I will."

Kate was up and off of the couch, ready to go. She followed him out of the room and down the hall. "Did you hear that? The guy was a cigar smoker, just like the creep in the bayou."

Mick liked her mind, among other things. "I wish she'd gotten a better look at him."

"No, I don't think you do. If this guy's the one who killed Otis, he wouldn't have risked having Mary Bell identify him. He knew about her cataracts, knew she couldn't make out his face. That means he and Otis were tight. Close enough to talk about family."

Mick pushed open the heavy wooden door and followed Kate out. She had a good point. Thank God for poor eyesight.

He unlocked the car and they climbed in. Mick fired the engine and turned the air conditioner on high. Opening the note, he read the address out loud. "Thirty-five Chelmette Road. Could be a place to stash stolen cars."

"Maybe it's the hangout for the theft ring…a chop shop."

"Whatever it is, we've got the key." He swung the piece of purple yarn with the key attached and picked up the radio microphone. "Dispatch, officer 557."

"557, go ahead."

"Run an identity check on an individual. One Alan Delancy, approximate age, twenty-five, last known address, New Orleans."

"Copy, 557, stand by."

"I wonder what will happen to Mary Bell now that Otis is gone?"

"That's assuming he was paying the bill on this place."

The radio crackled to life. "557. We show your individual disappeared in February '05. The individual's parents reported him missing on February 19."

"Copy that, dispatch. Is there a photo of the individual on file?"

"That's affirmative."

"Officer 557, clear." Mick replaced the handset and leaned back into the seat. "Did you ever get a look at Thomas Romaro?"

"No."

"Let's assume they knew each other. That's how Romaro was able to get close to Otis. Romaro was fished out of the Mississippi in February, around the same time this Delancy kid goes missing. What if Otis and Delancy were both mixed up in the auto-theft ring? Schneider said Thomas Romaro was a dead end. There was identification on the body, so no further search was necessary, but what if Thomas Romaro is really Alan Delancy?"

"You're the cop. You figure it out."

He shot her a smile and pulled the handset. "Dispatch, 557."

"Copy, 557, go ahead."

"Can you put the Delancy file into Sergeant Schneider's hands ASAP along with the open case file on one Thomas Romaro, deceased?"

"Affirmative. Will you follow up?"

"Yes. 557 clear."

Mick sucked in a breath. "Let's see where this key takes us." He tucked it into his pocket and put the car in reverse. They had to get to Pennybrook. It was clear across town from Gretna, but it was a huge break.

The cobbles click-clacked under the tires as they drove along. Mick stopped at the gate and the same attendant greeted them. "Hope you enjoyed your visit."

"Thanks, it was very informative, but I'd like to know if you keep a list of who enters the premises and who leaves?"

The attendant looked annoyed. "This isn't a

prison, Officer. I only direct people to the residents they wish to visit."

"Can you tell me if you remember who came to visit Mary Bell Whittley in early April?"

"Hmm. I don't remember anyone coming, just the police when they gave her that unfortunate news about her son."

"Is this facility surrounded by a fence?"

"No, not the whole complex. Just the main entrance."

"Thanks." Mick rolled up his window. "For the amount of bucks going into that place, you'd think they'd have better security."

"Someone for Mary Bell to call."

"She's pretty great."

"I hope I can be half as lively when I'm her age."

"If I catch you back talking an assailant, I'll have to lock you up…for your own protection, of course." Mick glanced at her. The late-afternoon sun coming through the window turned her hair to glistening strands of dark molasses. Her smile was real, genuine. He tried to picture her at Mary Bell's age, and he could. He could see her there next to him, fifty years from now. Still laughing, still smiling.

She looked at him and he looked away, desperate to hide his thoughts from her uncanny perception. How much longer could he hold out before he reached the point of no return?

Mick realigned his focus. Better to think about the case than a life with Kate. He stepped down on the gas and brought the car to speed.

Otis had hidden something and the key was going to unlock a secret that could blow his whole case wide open. Quite possibly it would reveal the reason Otis was murdered.

"Had an interesting conversation with Schneider today."

"Really. He agreed to spiff up those uniforms?"

"Yeah, right after he pulls the FBI into my case, that'll be the next item on the agenda." He tossed her a glance and watched her stare into her lap, fists clenched.

The traffic light glared red and he braked, wishing he'd found another way to tell her. "I'm sorry, Kate."

"I could get sucked into their investigation. Prosecuted."

"Don't get in front of this. Schneider and I speculated on the crime. There's nothing to substantiate it yet."

"Talk sense, Mick."

"Money. We think there was money in the seats and your abductor's threat confirmed it. Durant will be back in town soon, and Schneider is counting on him to back the theory with hard evidence. He's willing to talk, but he wants protection."

"There you have it. If there was money in those cars and I was sitting on it when I drove them to Dallas, across state lines, I could go to prison."

He brushed her hand. "I won't let it happen. You didn't know what was going on. We can get you immunity for your testimony. I'll vouch for you." Mick wished he could ease the knot in the bottom of his stomach, but she was right. If the feds wanted to, they could drag her in.

Chapter Twelve

He clipped the tiny red wire, stripped its poly coat and twisted the ends together with a wire nut. A sense of pride festered in his chest as he eyed his accomplishment, a margin of contentment he hadn't felt in a long time.

Dropping his cigar onto the floor, he ground it out under his boot heel. It was simple really. A little C4 connected to a timer, an invisible beam to set it in motion when the time was right.

It was too bad he'd turned the car over to a blackmailing weasel like Otis Whittley; he never guessed it would come back five years later to bite him.

He gunned the rage that idled in his veins and his heart rate accelerated. It would all end today. It wasn't how he'd planned it, but Jacoby and Kate were getting too close to the truth.

Disappointment surged inside of him. He'd wanted Mick to suffer...live through the pain of watching Kate being torn away from him one agonizing breath at a time.

This little device would rob him of the pleasure, but it was better than getting caught.

He stuffed the bomb into a duffel bag. Time was short, according to the blip on his monitor.

THE SUN WAS LOW IN THE SKY when they reached Pennybrook. Kate eyed the rural-turned-suburban area and tried to imagine what it had been like in Mary Bell's youth. Subdivisions had taken over where cane once grew, but there were still patches of open space and she looked for a Chelmette Road sign.

"There it is." She spotted the remains of an old wooden plaque. A single nail hammered in the center of the board secured it to a rotten post.

He slowed and turned down the single-lane road. There was a small yellow house at the end of the drive. The shades were drawn, the grass overgrown.

"Look, over there." Her hand trembled on the door handle and she pulled it the minute the car stopped. A garage was visible amongst a field of tall weeds.

"Kate, come back here," Mick cautioned, but she ignored him. She'd already spotted the tire tracks through the weeds to the shed. She broke into a jog. The ancient doors were open, pushed to the sides with enough force to split the rusted hinges. She slowed, with Mick right behind her.

"We're too late." His comment hovered in her mind and her hope crashed.

"Let's look around, there might be something." She moved into the enclosure, surveyed the ground and looked into the grease-saturated soil for any indication of what had been inside.

"Tire tracks. There was a car in here. But I doubt it was ever a takedown shop. No tools of the trade. The workbench doesn't have any signs there was ever equipment on it." She brushed her finger through the dust on the filthy work top. Her heart rate slowed with disappointment. She turned and walked back outside. "See the tracks, just before they disappear into the weeds? There were two cars. I'd guess one pulled the other one away."

"Right on, tracker Kate."

She waved his comment aside. "Try genius. Genius." Scanning the area, she tried to find anything that could help them, help her. Something shiny lay in the grass. "Over here. It's a padlock."

Mick pulled a hankie out of his pocket and picked the lock up with it. "Looks like a pair of bolt cutters were used. We'll have tool marks."

"Yeah, who needs a key."

"There's only one way to find out." He took the key out of his pocket.

She watched it slide into the lock and pop the clasp. "This is it, Otis's hiding place. He went to a lot of trouble. You said he didn't have a record. He was clean until he took the mayor's car, so why was he hiding a car out here, away from the action?"

Kate went back into the garage, desperate to find something, anything. It needed a second look. Nuts and bolts were scattered around. Oil cans. She looked up into the rafters, draped with cobwebs. A sheet of plywood had been nailed between a couple of beams and a rickety ladder was propped against the platform.

"Have you got a flashlight?"

"Sure, but this place is clear. Whatever was here is gone, and so is our lead."

"Just get it." She heard the car door open then close and felt the cool flashlight in her hand before she turned to look at him. "I'm going up there."

"Where?" Mick looked up at the platform she pointed to.

"That ladder doesn't look safe."

"Not safe, but used." She turned the flashlight on and brought its beam to bear on the fourth rung. The light enhanced a dirty shoeprint.

"Well, what do you know." He moved closer.

"Whoever climbed up here was tall. He started to climb halfway up." She moved closer to the ladder.

"Be careful, Kate."

"I will." She looked at him, aware of her desire to kiss him. She flicked off the flashlight, shoved it into her pants and stepped onto the second rung, keeping her feet spread and flush with the sides of the uprights. "No sense tampering with evidence."

"You should have been a cop." He smiled up at her.

"I'd rather just try to outsmart one." Taking another step she worked her way to the top and braced high on the ladder so she could get a downward look at the top of the plywood.

She turned on the flashlight.

Years of dust caked the wood, but like clay it held an image, the design was clear. Her heart jumped as she studied the intricate pattern of grillwork. It had been removed along with the car it belonged to, was her guess, but it was the missing piece of the pattern that did strange things to her insides.

The piece of grillwork at Mick's house fit into the blank spot, she was sure. This was the car that had killed his family. Her stomach tumbled. Could she tell him? Would he even believe her? "Mick."

"Yeah."

"You need to come look at this." She moved down the ladder.

"What's up there, Kate?"

"A piece of the past...your past." She reached the end of the ladder and stepped down.

"What are you talking about? How did my past get in this gar—"

Mick charged up the ladder. "Flashlight?" He reached down and grabbed it from Kate, turned it on and focused on the image in the dust.

Waves of horror crashed through him and churned his insides like a riptide. He reached toward the blank spot; his hand shook. He tried to control it, but couldn't. Deliberately he touched the place where the metal should be, but wasn't. The missing piece was twenty-five miles away on his mantel.

The hot burn of tears stung the backs of his eyes, but he forced them dry. Relief, sorrow and rage, stirred in his mind and the knowledge congealed.

"It was here, Kate. It was here all the time. That's what Otis had on Copeland. A murder weapon."

She reached up and grasped his ankle, touching him, attempting to share his pain, somehow. He could feel the warmth in her hand, knew the sympathy in her heart. And to think he'd always suspected her family. How much time had he wasted on one stupid rumor?

"We need CSI out here. Copeland might have left something behind." Mick sobered, shelved his internal quagmire of emotions and shut off the flashlight. He savored a moment of darkness and said his final goodbyes.

"Why would Otis hide a car used in a hit-and-run?" He speculated out loud. "Was he behind the wheel that night?" He moved down the ladder, careful to avoid the latent footprints.

"I don't think so. What if he was blackmailing someone. The someone who was driving?"

"How would he get the car? The driver would have found a way to get rid of it, so how would Otis get it?"

Kate was next to him. He knew she was thinking, turning the mystery for examination just as one twisted a kaleidoscope.

"What would you do with a hot car, if you didn't want to get caught with it and you didn't want to have it found…ever?"

"I'd take it down." She looked straight at him.

"Suppose the driver, after the accident, had the same idea. So he got someone, say Otis, to take the car to the chop shop, but Otis decides to keep the car instead of dumping it. The driver doesn't know the job hasn't been done and Otis has a get-out-of-jail-free card if he needs it. He'd be able to use it if he got into a pinch."

"I like it, but either the driver found out or Otis got greedy, wanted too much money?"

"Beautiful and equipped with a brain." Mick put his arm around her and pulled her close. Like salve, her nearness soothed his wounds.

"Comes standard on this model."

Pulling his cell phone from his belt, he called downtown. "I've got a secondary crime scene out in Pennybrook." He rattled off the address and signed off. "They'll be here in forty-five. Want to wait it out?"

"Sure."

"Thank you."

"For what?"

"Being Kate Robear. Ex-car thief, repo agent and all-round smart woman."

"I'm not sure some of those are too great, but the truth is the truth."

He pulled her against him, unsure if he could hold out much longer. The nights shut up with her were torture. Somewhere on the wild ride they'd taken together, his heart had been compromised.

Did she feel this powerful bond, too? Was

that elusive emotion lodged inside her or did she still crave her love from the past, the man she'd had a child with?

"I want to tell you what I think."

"Fire away." He breathed in the slight floral scent of her hair and zoned out on the feel of her body next to his.

Kate turned in his arms, wanting his full attention. "If the driver has the car, which I'd suspect, he'd take it down ASAP, assuming he just got hold of it. But if he got the location on the car a month ago, before he killed Otis…we're after a pile of scrap."

Her words sobered him and the intoxicated gleam in his green eyes dimmed. "Mixed in with a hundred other piles of scrap."

"Yeah, but I can help you find the right pile, Mick. Give me a chance."

A tic jumped along his jawline, the pressure of his teeth working against each other. She had to convince him to accept her help. It was the only way. "Please."

"I'm an officer of the law. There's a line that exists between what I do and what you did. It can't be crossed."

"We're talking about information. Let me call my brother…it could mean the difference between finding the man who killed your family and letting him vanish with your life wrapped around his finger. Please, Mick, do it for me. For us."

Sucking in a breath of contentment, she settled against him, lost in the stillness that invaded the little garage they stood in. Twilight had settled around them. The lights of the city glowed, reached into the night sky and cast a blanket of security around them. There wasn't anywhere else she wanted to be right now except with him.

He pulled her chin up and she could see the look of defeat in his eyes. "Okay. I want this bastard more than I care about the line. Make the call." He held his cell phone out to her.

She took it and turned away from him, wandering into the corner of the garage to press in Frank's number. She prayed he could get the information that would set them both free.

Mick listened to her muffled words as she spoke into the phone, heard her say goodbye to Frank, and move toward him. He was tired. Too tired to fight it anymore. Maybe it would take a Robear to find a killer, but the payoff would be justice. Wasn't that what he wanted?

Flicking on the flashlight he swept the garage with the beam in precise increments. They had time to kill before CSI arrived and it couldn't hurt to take another look.

In his peripheral vision he caught a glimpse of a red glow next to the entrance.

Reality slammed into his brain and took his breath with it. He drew the flashlight beam onto the electronic device at the opening to the garage.

Digital numbers glowed red, like the fires of hell…six…five…four…

Chapter Thirteen

"Run! Kate!" The seconds ticked in his brain. He grabbed her hand and sprinted out of the garage.

"Bomb!" The word came out as a guttural cry; he pulled her onto the ground next to the car and covered her body with his.

He could almost hear the last second die on the clock....

The blast exploded like the top of a volcano and split his eardrums. It reached out for them with fingers of fire.

"I'll protect you," he whispered against her hair.

The earth rocked. A wave of heat blew over his body. He held her tighter while pieces of flaming debris rained from the heavens and trailed smoke against the darkened sky. The garage was an inferno. It popped and hissed as flames devoured its skeletal remains.

Mick rolled onto his back and sucked in a

breath, still holding Kate's trembling body next to his. "Are you okay?"

"Warm, but alive."

He cradled her head and breathed in the scent of her hair, thankful to have her in his arms. His attention focused for a moment on the undercarriage of the car that had acted as a shield and saved their lives. The silhouette of an object attached to the underside caught and held his attention. Caution slipped through his veins. The flashlight was next to him. He turned it on and shone it at the device.

LoJack. They were being tracked.

MICK SAT UP IN THE CHAIR and looked at the illuminated dial on his watch. Three o'clock in the morning. In two more hours they'd have to move. It was risky to bring Kate here, to his home, but he'd taken every precaution to make it safe. Officers Nelson and Tassano had played the decoy game after the explosion and driven his bugged car to the station. They'd even promised to turn his office light on, in case the creep was watching.

These precious hours belonged to them... alone.

The glow from the VCR display touched Kate's face and cast it in pale green. Her eyes were closed. She lay on her side, one hand shoved under the pillow her head was on, the other dangling off the couch. They were safe for the moment. He'd parked the unmarked police car a block away. They'd taken the back alley to the house. All the blinds were closed and he hadn't turned on a single light.

Mick rubbed his face and sat back in the chair. This was no life. Running. How long before Kate could no longer stand to be separated from Cody? Motherly instinct was a strong force. Already, he'd seen her mood darken. He was losing her and he'd only just found her.

"A penny for your thoughts." Her voice startled him.

"With prices today, a penny isn't going to get you much, sweetheart." He saw a seductive glitter in her eyes, coupled with a sexy half smile, and he rode the wave of desire that surged inside of him. It was wrong to want her. Wrong to need her on a primal level he could barely keep caged. She was a witness, he was her protector, but he couldn't stop looking at her, couldn't control the thunder of his heart.

"I'll up it to a dime." Her voice was soft in the darkness of the room, coaxing.

He got up from the chair and moved to her

side. "Sold, but I don't know if you want to hear more of the same. It's going to include running."

She took his hand and pulled him down onto the couch.

Mick relaxed and let her touch excite him.

"It's how we're staying alive. It counts for something, but I agree, life on the move scrambles your brain. Maybe we should forget about it and focus on something else."

Her smile warmed his blood. "What did you have in mind, Ms. Robear?"

Kate pulled his hand to her lips and kissed it. Wrapped in the silence around them, it was possible to put her fears aside and give herself over to the whims of her heart. Need clawed through her, bolstering her desire for the man next to her. She wanted his hands on her skin, craved the intimate knowledge of his body while they satisfied each other.

He lowered his mouth to hers. The warmth in his lips penetrated her. She kissed him back and felt his need ratchet up. Lusty moans tumbled deep in his throat and he pulled back. She studied him in the dim light.

"Are you sure, Kate?"

"Are you?" She watched him hang his head, before he looked at her again. His breathing was heavy, his eyes smoldering with need. She wanted him, but she hesitated.

"You're so beautiful." He reached to cup the side of her face and sent a rush of heat through her body. She turned into his palm, kissing his fingers one by one.

He let out a sigh and she felt him tremble as he slid his fingers into her hair. "Did I mention sultry and irresistible?"

"No." She plunged into dangerous territory and brushed his cheek with her hand. The contact sent fire into her veins and she stared into his face. "Can you resist?"

His answer came in a kiss. Her heart pounded in her chest as he parted her lips with his tongue and explored her mouth. Her body hummed, her mind wrapped around one inescapable thought. She was falling in love with Mick Jacoby.

He scooped her into his arms. She put aside the last of her doubts and settled against him as his footsteps carried them closer to ecstasy. Closer to a release of the passion that had always been between them. She'd given her heart to him a piece at a time, now she would give him her body.

Mick moved along the hallway relishing the feel of Kate against him. Every nerve in his body pulsed. He felt as though he was emerging from a long hibernation. He moved into the bathroom and closed the door. Gently he stood her on her feet and found her lips in the darkness. "Do you like water?"

"Are you in it?"

"I will be, but there's some business I have to take care of."

He fiddled for the towel on the towel bar and pulled it off. Finding the door he laid the towel down, and shoved it into the crack at the bottom. "We can't be too careful."

"Uh-huh." She pulled his T-shirt out of his waistband. He didn't resist, but he wanted to see her and darkness wasn't going to rob him of the pleasure. "This is the only room in the house without a window." Reaching inside the medicine cabinet, he found the lighter and flicked it. Warm light invaded the small space and he touched it to the wick of the candle he had on the counter.

"I didn't know you were a romantic."

"There's a lot you don't know about me." He stared into her eyes while he worked the buttons on her blouse. Her gaze never wavered. The accelerated beat of her heart beneath his fingertips jumped and jived with his own. Undoing the last button, he slid her shirt off her shoulders and let it hit the floor. Making love to her was going to be the sweetest thing he'd ever done. "Shower?"

"Oh, yeah." She smiled up at him, pulled his T-shirt over his head and dropped it.

Mick breathed in her scent as it filled the small space. He watched her reach behind her back and pop the clasp on her bra. Reaching out he pulled the straps down and let the undergarment slip away.

Candlelight caressed the swell of her exposed breasts as she drew in one ragged breath after another. He closed his eyes, pulled her against him and stroked the tip of her nipple. "I need you. I've always needed you."

The admission rang true in his own ears. He needed her in his life, in his heart, in his bed.

She arched against him, rocketing his libido into overdrive. The tension turned unbearable as she undid the button on his pants and pulled the zipper down.

She stared into his eyes. He could see the glow of pleasure warming her cheeks to pink, but questions danced in her eyes.

"I'm your witness, Mick. What's the penalty if we get caught?"

The question forced his desire down a notch, but it skyrocketed again as she brushed his chest with her hands.

"My job, my reputation."

"What about your heart?" Her expression

was pleading in the candlelight, her body a vision he would never forget or ever stop wanting, but she was giving him a choice.

Where was his heart? He could feel the erratic beat deep in his chest. His resistance crashed and he pulled her to him. "I want you, Kate."

In slow time he popped the buttons on her Levi's one by one. He heard a sigh in her throat as he slid his hand into her panties. He found her lips, kissing the sigh away, stoking the burn that would soon meld them together.

Every inch of his body wanted her as he lowered his head to her breast and took her nipple in his mouth. She pushed her fingers into his hair and he heard a sigh from deep in her throat.

Sliding his hand around onto Kate's bottom, he worked her pants down. Her skin was smooth, like fine powder. He hardened and fought for control as he pushed her pants down with his foot and shoved his slacks off.

A charge hung in the air around them. He moved the candle onto a shelf and lifted Kate onto the counter. Reaching into the medicine cabinet he pulled out an unopened box of condoms.

"Let me." Kate took the box, a sultry smile on her lips.

"Better check the expiration date."

She tipped the box to the candlelight. "A month left. It's our lucky night."

He stared into her eyes as she rolled a condom onto his shaft. His breathing went unchecked, his pulse hummed inside of his body so hard he thought he'd explode.

She opened her legs for him and he pushed into her.

She moaned as he drove deeper, cupping her hips with his hands. He slicked with her wetness. She was tight around him, silky. He thrust into her again and again, establishing a rhythm that sent wave after wave of pleasure through him.

Ecstasy turned him white-hot. He could feel her climax rising with his, her soft moans of pleasure driving him deeper inside of her. Mick closed his eyes and pumped her, feeling her come to orgasm. She clawed his back, whispering his name. He kissed her, still stroking.

He couldn't hold on any longer. A deep thrust and he came. Pleasure overwhelmed his thinking and sucked the last of his energy from his body.

He stayed inside her in the afterglow, kissing her lips, her forehead, her neck, breathing in the sweet perfume of her body.

"It's been a long time."

Gently, he pulled out of her, holding her against him, stroking her hair, her cheek. "So much for the myth, single people have lots of sex. You've just broken my monkish streak."

Her chuckle was soft. "They say married couples do it the most."

Mick thought of his relationship with Natalie. It had been good, but he'd never made love to her like this, or experienced the volume of emotional satisfaction he felt right now. He wished the memories away. Back into the past where they'd come from. Far away from the woman in his arms. He'd always considered them lost treasure, to be dug up. Now he buried them, forever.

Kate snuggled against him, feeling wisps of passion stir inside her again. She could feel the effect of love, but the words were lost to her. The last tether she'd tied on her heart, pulled away.

"Can I interest you in a shower by candle-light?" His voice was low, sexy, suggestive.

"If I get to use the soap first."

He released her and turned on the faucets. She drank in the hard lines of his body where the soft light touched it. The idea of sudsing him from head to toe and in between, excited her. He was the most beautiful man alive she decided as she hopped off the counter and took his hand. He smiled at her and her heart squeezed in her chest. She stepped into the tub with him and grabbed the soap.

HE LEANED AGAINST the streetlight and cast a glance at the lit window in the police station. Mick's office. He could visualize Mick and Kate inside, huddled together, squirming with fear. The image pounded deep down into his brain and he smiled.

Lucky…they'd been lucky. The bomb he'd planted hadn't blown them to bits. The game was still on.

Dropping the butt of his cigar, he ground it into the sidewalk and pretended it was Jacoby's head. Turning, he pushed into the stream of night owls flocking the street.

KATE STAYED CLOSE to Mick as they moved down the alley, sticking to the shadows. They'd made love again and stayed in the shower too long. She felt like a prune, but her heart was happy.

The first rays of dawn were already stretched out to touch the darkness.

They made it to the car and got inside. Kate pulled the baseball cap she'd donned down a little farther. She hated feeling as though there was always someone watching her, but she decided to ignore it. This would end someday. Soon she would be with Cody again, the creep making her life crazy would be locked up, and

Mick… She chanced a glance his way. Where would he be in the scheme of her life? She knew in her gut where she wanted him to be, but would love be enough to keep them together? Was her former life of crime and an FBI investigation going to sabotage their happiness?

She focused on the road as they pulled away from the curb. It was early. Five-thirty in the morning. The street was quiet, some houses had their lights on, but for the most part the neighborhood slept.

"Do you want to see it, Kate?"

Instinctively she knew what he meant, and she thought about the piece of grillwork she'd taken off the mantel this morning and slipped into her pocket. "Yeah. Let's go."

Mick flipped a U-turn in the street and headed back toward the house, then turned onto a side street, pulled along the curb and stopped the car.

She climbed out first, sensing his hesitancy. Stepping around to the front of the car, she stopped and waved him out.

He shut the car door and leaned against it. "I used to drive past here every day, until I couldn't anymore. I started taking another route so I could avoid looking down this street. This is the first time I've been here in years. They were hit in the crosswalk, there." He pointed back toward the main road.

"No eyewitnesses. The cops figure the folks on the corner across the street would have seen something, but it was a Saturday night and no one was home."

Kate eyed the brick facade next to the car and the one on the other side of the narrow street. It felt as if a tunnel stretched the entire length of the block. The tall expanses would have prevented a good view from any direction. She tried to visualize what Natalie and Megan must have seen, but the image made her sick. There had been no escape.

"It was late that night. There was a street fair going on a couple of blocks down. Natalie loved cotton candy and the excitement. She was determined that Megan got in on some of the fun. I'd pulled six ten-hour shifts that week. I was beat. I told them to go. Just go and have fun. I kissed them and gave them a hug...that was the last time I saw them alive."

"I'm sorry, Mick. Sorry you lost them." She moved in close to him and touched his hand.

His arms went around her. "Me too, but I found you." His head came down and he kissed her, pulling back too soon.

"The next day I found the piece of grillwork

at the end of the street in that storm drain." He motioned down the corridor.

"Who'd have thought it would go that far?"

"You never know what can happen at an accident scene. Kinetics make the impossible, possible."

She patted the metal in her pocket. She hadn't told him she had it. She didn't know if he'd prepared himself to see it fit into place, that was if they could get their hands on the actual piece of grillwork it had come from.

The music of her cell phone played inside her backpack. She slid the zipper and pulled out her phone. "Hello."

"Kate? It's Frank. I've got your information but you're probably too late."

She watched Mick lean against the rear of the car and look away. His closure was dependent on this and so was hers. "Give it to me."

"The buzz is a Porsche 944 went to a chopper about two weeks ago. It was a weird takedown and nobody wants to talk about it. There's one person who seems to be in the know."

"Who?"

"Dylan Talbot."

Kate's emotions did a somersault and landed right side up. "Is he involved?"

"No…not directly, but he knows the takedown artist. He set him up. Seems he's branching out. Word is nobody gets to the guy without going through him."

"Thanks. Any word on the hot pink Jag seats?"

"Yeah. Your boy bought them at an aftermarket shop out in Kenner. The guy claimed the old seats in maroon leather were slashed up by his girlfriend after she found a pair of panties in the glove box that weren't hers."

"That's a tall one."

"There's more. My buddy took the frames as a trade-in. He found a couple of twenty-dollar-bill corners clamped in the springs."

"No kidding."

"Would I lie to you? I don't like the smell of this, Katie. If that was stolen drug money somebody is going to want it back. Anyone who touched that ride is a target and those guys don't screw around."

"I know. I'll be careful." She looked at Mick, who'd taken an interest in the conversation.

There was a long pause at the other end of the line. "Just come back to us. Mom's doing so much better with Cody here. He's good for us all."

Heat pressed into her cheeks and she looked at Mick, who'd moved to her side. "I will… soon. How is he?"

"Great, but he misses you."

"Tell him I miss him, too."

"Will do. By now."

The call ended and she rode out a surge of mixed emotions. The burn of tears stung her eyes, her throat squeezed, but she held on.

"Oh, babe. You can do this." Mick put his arms around her and pulled her close. She sucked in the warmth of him next to her, letting his nearness soothe the ache. "I know I can, but how much longer will this last?"

"I don't know. We'll get the other guy...soon. I promise."

Mick's heartbeat was steady underneath her ear and she pulled confidence from him. She had her child. His was gone. She could do this. She could hold on with everything she had.

"It's Dylan. He knows who chopped the Porsche 944. Frank says we need to use him as a way in."

"You're sure?"

"Yeah, but the car went to pieces weeks ago." Disappointment flooded his face and his jaw muscles clenched.

"There's got to be something left. Let's go find it." Mick started back to the car, holding Kate's hand.

The sound of a revved engine made his nerves

jump. He scanned for the source of the sound, but it was too late.

The Honda was on them.

A flash of black that closed the gap at fifty miles per hour.

Chapter Fourteen

With every ounce of energy he had, Mick slung Kate toward the sidewalk.

The edge of the car's bumper caught the back of his left leg as he fought to escape death. He slammed to the pavement.

Pain shot through him. He gritted his teeth and clawed his way into the gutter.

The brake lights of the car glowed red, tires smoked, squealing as the driver tried to take the turn too fast. He overshot and crashed into a utility pole.

Sparks flew, dropped and hissed to the ground.

The blare of the horn split the early-morning air.

Mick closed his eyes. It was over. Then, like a vivid dream, she was next to him. Brushing her hand over his cheek, soothing the agonizing pain that invaded his body and took his mind.

He focused on her touch. Latched onto it like a pain pill and pulled himself onto the curb.

"He tried to kill you, Mick." She motioned to the crushed car, the outline of the driver slumped over the wheel shown under the streetlight.

"I won't die that easy, Kate, but it looks like he's not going anywhere. We've got him and his partner. You're going to get your life back." He looked into her face and witnessed a brief look of disappointment. The emotion portrayed on her face lodged in his heart like a knife. She didn't need him anymore.

KATE CLIMBED INSIDE the car and Mick slid in next to her. It was a miracle he'd escaped serious injury. The EMTs on scene had wrapped his bruised and battered leg and released him with an order to go to the E.R., ASAP. The driver of the car was on his way to the hospital and then to a jail cell.

Pumping her bravado, she tried to work up her courage. Mick had been able to play to Dylan's ego when he thought they were just looking for some action. Giving up a chopper was going to be a different story. These guys were tight and they rarely ratted each other out.

"Dylan is going to stonewall you."

"How do you figure?" He fired up the engine and pulled away from the curb.

"You're going to ask him for information he'll guard with his life. There's a code of silence you can't crack."

"I respect that, Kate, but I'm going to use whatever means I have to."

A fit of nerves jumped along her spine. "Just be careful. If you put him in a corner he'll fight."

"Thanks." He touched her hand.

"There's more." Kate lumped her courage. "Frank located the shop where Durant got the seats. His trade-ins were slashed up and the springs were pinching the corners of some twenty dollar bills. The seats were full of money. You have your evidence."

He squeezed her hand, but it did little to stem her fear.

"I'll talk to Schneider. I'll bare my soul. We'll get you a deal."

She looked at him as he focused on the road. Could he hold the FBI back?

They drove to Dylan's shop in silence and whipped into the parking lot. Kate spotted Dylan in the corner at his workbench, his back to them. Caution hitched to her thoughts as Mick jumped out of the car and limped toward him. Not even an injury could dampen his zeal.

Dylan whirled around. "Wait a damn minute, you can't come in here. Who do you…"

"Wanna bet? This badge says I can." Mick flashed his shield.

The color drained from Dylan's face. "You're a cop?" He glared at her. "You stupid bitch. You brought the heat down?"

"Dylan! Shut up and listen." She leveled her best wise-up look on him. "We need information about a chop job."

"Go to hell." He spat the words, but his eyes went large when Mick grabbed his shirt and shoved him backward.

"Meet you there, but not until you tell us what we want to know. There was a questionable takedown on a Porsche 944. Rumor is, you know about it."

Dylan's eyes glazed over with determination. Kate remembered his stubborn tendencies. How were they going to get him to roll over?

She moved in on the two men. "Come on, Dylan. It's not like you don't know. You've got contacts all over this town. I know how good you are, they'll never know it came from you. Besides, it's already done. We'd just be on a treasure hunt. In need of a few parts."

Mick shot her a why-didn't-you-consult-me

look and glared at Dylan. "That's right, it'll stay right here."

"Arrest me, dude. I'm not saying a word. I want my lawyer."

"You SOB." Mick shoved him again.

Dylan turned, grabbed a lug wrench from the counter and lunged at Mick. "You're going to be sorry."

Kate hustled out of the way as the two men grunted and tussled like a couple of bulls, but her heart stopped when she saw Dylan reach for Mick's gun. "Your gun!"

He grabbed Dylan's hand, let an uppercut fly and caught him in the face. He stumbled back and dropped the lug wrench.

"Stop it! Both of you." She put herself between them. "Dylan. Jake and I have a son."

Surprise replaced the anger on Dylan's face as he dabbed at his bloody nose with his shirtsleeve.

"Someone wants us dead. If it weren't for Officer Jacoby, I wouldn't be here."

"I'm an uncle? Jakie's a father…why didn't you tell me, Kate? Why did you just disappear, run away?"

She looked into his face and saw real questions. A man struggling to understand. "For Cody. I didn't want this life for him." She raised her hands, palms up. "You think I wanted to lie awake at night wondering if he'd come home? Was he sitting in jail or lying in the morgue? I ran away from this, and my family, because I want better. I deserve better.

"Do you want to see him?" She felt like a balloon with its air let out. Fishing in her backpack, she pulled out her wallet and opened it to a picture of Cody. "He looks like Jake, don't you think?"

Dylan took the wallet and stared at the picture for a long time. "My buddy over in Kenner called a few weeks back. He found a '97 Porsche 944 in his lot with a note on the steering wheel, telling him to take it down immediately. There was twenty grand in the glove box."

He handed the wallet back to her and turned to his bench, bracing his hands on the countertop. "You might get a souvenir. I'll call him and tell him I'm sending over a couple of shoppers. He's on the corner of Cypress and Cranston. Hank's Garage."

Kate's heart leaped into her throat. "Thank you."

Mick took her hand, just as Dylan turned around.

"Kate?"

"Yeah."

"Can you bring him around sometime?"

"I will." She turned away and left the garage with Mick.

The morning air was already gathering humidity; it pressed down on her with a vengeance, but she felt charged up. Exposing secrets long hidden felt good. She recounted the times she'd sworn Jake to secrecy about Cody. Her family, too, had been left out, all so she could protect her son and pretend her past didn't exist.

"That was a crazy scene back there. I've never watched a man be disarmed by a picture before."

She jerked him to a stop next to the car. "Dylan is Cody's uncle and he has a right to get to know him. So does my family. I may not like what they did for a living, but they're still my family." She chewed her words, finding they had substance but not much flavor. She'd have to rethink her decision to disappear and try to come to terms with it.

"I've seen you disarmed by a snapshot." She fixed her gaze on him. "When you look at those photos on your mantel, you're moved. They were your family, your life. You can't change that, any more than you can change what happened to them. You can only deal with it. I'm no different. I pretended my family was dead, but they're not. I have to make peace, somehow."

"Come on, Kate. I didn't mean to stir the pot." Mick took her shoulders and she saw understanding in his eyes. "I haven't been able to find a damn thing on the Robears."

"Let's go shopping."

Mick had never heard of Hank's Garage, but then he only had knowledge on a handful of choppers. They could pack up in a matter of hours and disappear into the New Orleans night without a trace. It paralleled a ghost hunt.

"About last night." He started the car and pulled away from the curb. "Things were pretty heated... I like to take my time, but I needed you, and you were so... damn...hot."

She touched his thigh and a jolt of pleasure equal to the memory hissed through his body.

"Nothing like making love to calm your frustration." She rubbed his thigh and sent his control into outer space.

"Damn, woman. I'm trying to drive." Pushing his desire back, he focused on the road. "What do you think our chances are of finding the remains of the car?"

"Fair to good. Everything that's worth anything gets saved. The motor parts are probably gone, those get snapped up right away. Things like headlights, grillwork, windows and hardware stay around longer. We've got a chance."

He touched her hand and drew on the energy that the contact gave him. "Thanks in advance."

"You're welcome."

"I just hope we can find the grill. Our guy must have touched it when he took it down from the rafters. With any luck his prints will be all over it."

"What if he wore gloves?"

"You always ask the hard questions, don't you, Kate?" He squeezed her hand and released it. "I'll still be closer than I was five years ago."

"Who else knows about the grillwork you found in the storm drain?"

"Nobody. Legally, I should have turned it over as evidence, but I couldn't let it go. Lockup is good, but evidence gets miscatalogued and lost. I couldn't risk it."

"I would have done the same thing. So, it's okay if I brought it along?"

He looked at the scrap of metal she held out like an offering and his throat tightened. "It's been on the mantel too long."

"Change, Mick. Change is good. It's getting there that turns you inside out."

He shot her a smile and squeezed the steering wheel. He had changed since she'd stolen into his life and robbed him of his heart.

They whizzed past the outskirts of Kenner

and took exit ten. Mick turned down Cypress Street and crept past Hank's Garage, scooping out the location. He pulled into a parking space half a block away and killed the engine.

"I don't suppose I can convince you to stay in the unit, listen to the radio, do your nails?" He wanted her in the car, out of the way of danger.

"Not a chance."

"I didn't think so. Here's the deal." He climbed out of the car and moved toward the garage with Kate next to him. "Let me do the talking. This guy could be dangerous. If your buddy Dylan called ahead, we're in clean, if not…"

Kate's stomach fisted. "I'm sure he called. He knows the kind of trouble I'm in. I could always trust his word." She prayed they didn't walk into a trap. Most choppers were seedy, but they weren't killers, just mechanics who'd found another way to put welders to work for fun and profit. She'd been around the type her whole life.

"Okay, babe, time to suck up to your daddy."

She put her arm around his waist and enjoyed the close contact. "Just a couple of starstruck lovers looking to buy hot Porsche parts. How romantic."

"It could be." Mick brushed her cheek with his finger. The caress flashed her mind back to last night and a shiver of delight moved through her.

"Time to get serious." He opened the shop door and they walked inside.

The odor of oil and tires was heavy. A haze of smoke hung in the air a foot or so from the ceiling. It was how she remembered it from the old days, walking into Dylan's shop after a job. A night of doing what takedown artists do best.

"Hey." A man in gray coveralls stepped out from behind a shiny blue Dodge pickup. "You Dylan's friends?"

"Yeah."

"He put the word in for you. Come out back. I've got a hell of an assortment. Anything in particular you're after?"

"I'd like to build up a 1997 Porsche 944 for my girlfriend." He grinned down at her. "The one I've got is minus its grill."

"All right."

They followed him out of the rear door to the junkyard. "All my Porsche stuff is on this fence wall. Help yourself."

"Thanks, man. Do you see anything that catches your eye, sweetie?"

Kate broke away from him. "I don't know." She meandered along, scanning the neat stacks of stolen merchandise. Choppers could be over-protective of their parts and she didn't want to raise Hank's suspicions by diving in uncontrollably. She let her gaze slip over the grills, trying to look disinterested, but one leaning against the wall caught her attention and quickened her pulse. "What about this?" She picked it up and held it out in front of her. "It's missing a little piece." She put her finger through the hole and wiggled it at Mick. "But that's okay, it gives it character. What do you think?"

"It could work. Are you sure there isn't a better one, honey?"

She smiled at him. "My money, or should I say, your money is on this one. Pay the man."

"How much?" Mick pulled out his wallet.

"Hundred bucks?"

"Sold." He fished the money out of his wallet and handed it over. "Good doing business with you."

"Likewise. If you need anything else, just let me know."

"I've got a couple of buddies putting together a 97—mind if I send them your way?"

"Hell no. I need the business."

"I'll call them this morning. They'll be over here in a flash." He gave her a "let's go" nod and they left the garage. Kate interlocked her fingers with his as they walked toward the car.

"I can't believe I just left there and didn't try

to stop him from cutting up that truck. You've corrupted me, Kate."

"Bull. You've got nothing but good in your bones, Mick Jacoby. Besides, you don't know he's going to chop it. He's got a chest full of tools. Maybe he's wrenching on it."

"Yeah, and I'm the Queen of England."

"Let it go. We got what we came for."

He opened the trunk; she laid the grill inside, dusted off her hands and pulled the metal out of her pocket. "You need to do it?" She handed it to Mick, watching tension play along his jaw. His eyes were bright with excitement.

Mick's hand shook as he put the piece into place, rejoining the inanimate objects that had torn his world apart. "I can't believe it. All these years I kept this hunk of metal. I knew it would fit somewhere, but I never guessed it would lead me to you." He kissed her, lost in the moment. Closure was so close he could touch it. With Kate in his life there wasn't anything he couldn't do.

"Let's get this to the lab. If the driver touched it, I'm going to know." He pulled his cell phone and keyed in Tank McCray's number.

"Tank? Jacoby here. I need you and Ricky to go on a scavenger hunt. There's a chop shop at Cypress and Cranston. Dude's name is Hank. I put the word in for you. I want every scrap piece you can find for a '97 Porsche 944. Anything that might give us a print or paint flakes. Get it to the lab, have Derrick Callahan put a rush tag on it. I want answers by this afternoon. Play it cool. My informant can't take any heat on this. Thanks." He ended the conversation and turned toward Kate.

"Have time for brunch with a really hungry man?"

"Oh yeah."

Mick fired up the car engine. Excitement gnawed his nerves and knotted in his gut. They had the car, all they needed was the driver. There had to be a fingerprint somewhere on the scrap. He cast a glance toward Kate. "I know what you did back at Dylan's was hard." He looked back at the road.

"It was worth it. I've been running away for a long time, but I think I've finally found my way back."

"Would that be the truth, Kate? Because it's always gotten me through."

"The truth feels good."

He knew what felt good and she was sitting next to him. His appetite surfaced, but it wasn't going to be satisfied with food.

JACOBY WAS UP TO SOMETHING. He brought the spotting scope down. His car was parked where it had been all night, but didn't they have to eat? He moved around the small room, puffing on his cigar. Was it possible he'd found the bug?

Mick wasn't that smart; he could think circles around the bastard and tie him in knots.

No, they were just late risers. Sleeping upright in a chair was hell on the back. He moved to the window again and focused the scope on the front of the police station. Nothing.

He glanced at his watch. Two o'clock. They had to come out sometime. Raising the scope again, he scanned the people on the sidewalk. *Wait.* He pulled his attention back to a couple of guys walking toward the front entrance. They both wore ball caps and dark glasses. One hung slightly back. He was shorter, more feminine.

He rolled the focus to full power, zooming in on the guy's shoes. Black running shoes, the kind Kate wore.

Anger ignited inside of him. He focused on the lead man. There was no mistake. He watched the leisurely stroll he'd seen a hundred times.

Rage fired through him and burned the last threads of his sanity. It was time. Time to bring Kate into his world. Time to crush her in front of Mick's eyes. He'd use the hands-on approach. It would be more satisfying than a dark street and a stolen car.

MICK SLID HIS CHAIR close to Schneider's desk and set his coffee cup down. "What did you say?"

"Your witness, where is she?"

"In my office catching up on her e-mail." Mick didn't like the look on Schneider's face, the tension around his jawline, or the lack of eye contact. He wasn't his jovial self.

"Why?"

"Just checking. I want to commend you on the heads-up regarding Thomas Romaro aka Alan Delancy. His folks were able to identify him with the autopsy photos.

"I'm glad someone gets some closure. Anything out of the driver of the black Honda?"

"He admitted to the break-in at Kate's house and trying to run you down. He's facing attempted murder charges, he's made a deal with the D.A. Said Otis told him he was blackmailing David Copeland. Any idea with what?"

"A Porsche 944 for starters. The same car used in the hit-and-run that killed Nat and Megan." Mick's emotions twisted.

"Copeland was the driver. Are you sure?"

"Looks that way."

"We know Copeland's working both ends of the money-laundering scam, distribution of the cars and acquisition." Schneider flipped open a file and scooped up a sheet of paper. "Hot off the fax this morning." He handed it to Mick. "My buddy at the bureau sent it. Looks like we've got our crime."

Mick looked over the information. "That's slick." He leaned back in his chair, considering the operation. He didn't like the way Ben eyed him then looked away. "What is it? Did I miss something?"

"Any chance Ms. Robear knew what she was doing? Copeland was her boss, too, and he's playing both ends."

"No, and just because her name is Robear doesn't mean she's guilty by association."

"You've changed your tune."

"I know it for a fact. She's clean."

"We're not talking pocket change. The FBI's investigation has uncovered ten-million reasons for her to get involved."

"Ten million? In the cars Kate repossessed?" Mick thought of the slashed seats in the Beamer. Otis had double-crossed Copeland by discovering the money and tried to exchange it for the Porsche.

The FBI has been monitoring an outfit called

Abacus Motors for the last couple of months. They're on the verge of shutting the operation down and rounding up the suspects, but before you chase out of here, Mick, I have something to tell you."

"Let's have it."

"This came in from the lab an hour ago. Tank and Ricky got your car parts and trashed the department's budget."

"The price of crime fighting?" He felt the undercurrent in the room turn serious.

"That's not the half of it." Ben's demeanor softened and he looked Mick straight in the eyes. "Callahan pulled prints off the driver's side window and the rearview mirror. Good prints. We got some paint flakes, too, and made a match with the flakes we recovered from the...bodies."

His heart rate increased and he tried to force the mental images of that night into oblivion.

"We ran them through AFIS, nothing. I took a chance and pushed them in-house. We got a match."

He leaned toward Schneider. A charge built in the air around them.

"The match is sitting upstairs in your office. The prints belong to Kate Robear and this preliminary report confirms it." He shoved a file toward Mick.

Mick's heart slammed into his ribs and died on the jagged tips. The room fell like a runaway elevator, plunging into hell. He stood up and raked his hands over his head. It couldn't be true. "Are you sure?"

"I wish I wasn't, for your sake, but evidence doesn't lie. The old DMV records don't leave any doubt. She owned a 1997 Porsche 944. The paint color is a match. We've got enough to put her away."

"You want me to arrest her?" The idea made him sick, put a bomb in the pit of his stomach.

"I'm pulling you off this case."

"Dammit, Ben. You can't jerk this."

"It's a stretch, Jacoby. You quit homicide, you're working auto theft. You've got an emotional choke hold on this case. Draw some equal signs for me."

"I can't. Not yet." He stood up, his insides churned the emotions he'd been feeling toward Kate, but only one floated to the surface. Only one stayed where he could grab it, and he put it on like a life preserver. "What about Copeland? He's our guy. Otis was blackmailing him with the car."

"Maybe Copeland was taking care of it for Kate Robear."

"No way." Mick's guts twisted.

"Phone records led us to an address on

Copeland. The warrant is ten minutes out. Do you want in on this?"

"Yeah." He thought of Kate upstairs in his office. She was safe. Her stalkers were behind bars, and he wanted a piece of Copeland with a vengeance. "What's his location?"

"Bayou Gauche."

A blade of caution sliced up Mick's spine.

THE AFTERNOON HEAT in Bayou Gauche was oppressive. It settled on Mick's skin like a wet blanket as they closed in on Copeland's house. It was a lot of real estate, but the location gave Mick the creeps. He guessed it had been purchased with laundered money and the locality was intended to keep people away. There were no lights on, but then he hadn't expected there would be.

"New Orleans Police, open the door!" The entry team kicked it in and Mick followed them inside, struck by the pristine condition of the house. It didn't look lived-in. A scent of cigar smoke hung in the air and Mick realized its importance. Copeland had been there that night in the swamp, watching Kate.

One by one they swept the rooms. Each empty space weighted his heart. They had to arrest Copeland. He needed to dispel any link between Kate, Copeland and the Porsche.

"In here," an officer yelled.

Mick moved down the hallway.

"You've got to see this."

Stepping around him, Mick sucked in a breath. The walls of the room were plastered with pictures. Pictures of Natalie and Kate, Cody and Megan, interspersed with newspaper articles about the hit-and-run.

His brain tried to take in the sheer number and scope, but he couldn't. He tried to connect Copeland to the presence of the people in his life. A man he didn't know, sure seemed to know them.

Schneider let out a low whistle. "Dark obsession, I'd say. This guy is one sick puppy."

Mick looked at the pictures closely. The backgrounds and surroundings. Parks, the mall. "Public places, all of them." His gaze settled on a shot of Natalie and the blood stopped in his veins.

Their bedroom?

She was lying on the bed. He recognized the burgundy spread beneath her. Her smile was seductive, inviting.

He turned away, sickened by the reality. He hadn't taken the picture. "This doesn't make any sense, Ben. If Nat had known Copeland, I'd have seen it."

"He sure seems to know Kate."

Mick stared at the pair of lacy panties Ben held on the end of a pen. The panties Kate had described as missing from her house. "Trophy?"

"I'd say so."

He rubbed the back of his neck and glanced around the room. A snapshot of Kate was in his line of sight and he put his focus on her. Her smiling eyes and mouth, her values teetering somewhere between right and wrong, mostly right. He swallowed and turned to Schneider.

"Something about this is too easy. Look at these pictures. This guy's been at this for a long time. There's a personal element."

Mick turned around the room, his thoughts swimming in confusion. "Let's search the place. Find some verification on Copeland's identity." Mick followed Ben into the front of the house, where a gloved officer was already pulling paperwork out of a desk drawer. He paused and turned around.

"Check this out." The office laid a paper on the desktop.

Time stopped as Mick stared at the name on an unpaid power bill. The letters reached out and stole the air from his lungs.

"I'll be damned," Ben whispered next to him.

"Kate!" Before her name left his lips he burst out the front door, numb with reality.

David Copeland didn't exist, but Bret Byer did.

Chapter Fifteen

Kate smiled through her tears at the picture on Mick's computer screen.

Cody's digital image looked back at her with a giant, Happy Mother's Day logo underneath, compliments of her brother Frank. Her heart sagged in her chest and she wished her arms around him again. A month on the run, what had she missed?

The air pressure in the room changed as the door behind her opened and closed. It was well into the afternoon. Mick had promised they'd take a walk around the square.

"Mick, look at this, isn't it…" His hands were on her shoulders. Hot. Sticky. The acrid smell of cigar smoke entered her nose and set off an explosion in her mind.

Realization knifed into her. She tried to stand up, but he held her down and covered her mouth with his hand.

She tried to scream; he pressed harder.

"I've waited a long time for this, Kate," he whispered into her ear as he nuzzled her neck.

Her stomach lurched in revulsion as he dragged his rough fingers over her cheek. She turned away and closed her eyes. *Focus.* They were in the police station, for God's sake. If she could only scream a dozen cops would converge on them.

"I can tell you've been with him. You smell like sex."

Fear cut a hole in her, leaving horrible images to spill out. *Where are you, Mick?*

"Mick always shares with me, even if he doesn't know it." He snorted, deep and throaty. "We're going to leave here, Kate. Nice and quiet, and just in case you think you want to scream, don't. I've been watching him play outside your mother's house."

She stared at Cody's picture on the screen. Fear worked her into a panic. He knew where Cody was?

"He's a good kid. Safe for now, but you wouldn't want anything to happen to him, would you?"

"Uh-uh," she mumbled against his hand. In her peripheral vision, she saw the gleam of a knife blade. She held in a sob as he waved it in front of her face.

"My best knife. It would be an honor to break it in on your kid. Do you understand?"

Nodding, she blinked back tears.

"I'm going to take my hand off your mouth. If you scream, it'll be the last thing you ever do." He lowered his hand.

She tasted blood and swallowed. "Can I stand up?"

"Easy, sweetie."

The endearment angered her, but she searched for a cooldown. He would kill her if she gave him a reason. She glanced at her backpack on the desk. She had to have it.

"I'm turning around."

"Go ahead. You're going to be seeing a lot of me."

Slowly she raised her gaze to his face, a face she knew.

Bret Byer stood in front of her in battle stance. His dark blue shirt and pants, clean and pressed, a seductive smile on his thick lips.

"You're Bret Byer." She swallowed the lump in her throat and willed her heart to slow down. Sweat leached from her palms and her muscles instinctively tightened.

"In the flesh, or Copeland if you prefer. Hell, I'm anyone you want me to be."

He shoved the chair over, moved close to her

and pressed the knife blade to her throat. "You're so beautiful. Natalie was, too. Micky boy can pick 'em, but not this time." He stroked a lock of her hair and pulled it to his nose, breathing in deeply. "I've been waiting for so long."

She resisted the overwhelming need to jerk away. She could feel the blade against her skin, cool, deadly, knew her life hinged on the edge and dangled from the decisions she made in the next few minutes.

"I can hear your mind work, Kate." He dropped her hair, stepped back and slipped the knife into a case strapped to his belt. "Why do you think I picked you?"

"You picked me?"

"You're smart. You know how to think, to move. A bit of a challenge on the road to payback."

She fidgeted under his hypnotic stare. She could see the glow of insanity in his eyes. "Was Natalie Jacoby payback, too?"

His eyes narrowed, he circled her like a snake coiling around prey.

A shudder pulsed in her and rippled through her body. He was evil, dangerous.

"For a time. Until Mick stepped in and stole her back. I was screwing her up until then. The best part was, she wanted me instead of him."

Kate pulled in a breath, trying to release the ache she felt for Mick, for what he'd suffered at the hands of Byer, a man he'd trusted with his life.

He snorted. "Natalie is old news. You and I are going to make new sounds together. Satisfying sounds." He touched her cheek again. "Gotta go. Get your cap and sunglasses."

The Ray-Ban shades were lying next to her backpack. She picked up the cap, put it on and pushed her hair inside of it. Slowly she picked up her backpack, but he caught her arm.

"You don't need that."

"You want me to look natural, don't you?"

He snatched the backpack from her and yanked down the zipper. Staring inside, he gave it a shake and zipped it shut. "Here." He thrust the bag at her.

Cautious relief spread through her as she slipped her arms into the straps, securing the lifeline to her body. Folding the sunglasses, she clutched them in her hand, while her knees went to jelly.

Byer was standing with his hand on the doorknob, a dark blue cap on his head and a pair of shades on. "Remember, I know where he is.

"Please, don't hurt him."

"Behave."

Nodding, she moved through the door into the hallway, wishing Mick's office was in the middle of the main entrance instead of the corner of the building. There was no one in the corridor. She glanced at the clock on the wall: 3:30 p.m.

"Over here." He motioned to the service elevator and pressed the button. It opened and she stepped through the door, straining to hear the pounding of shoes. The echo of voices was all around them. She prayed they would have to pass someone, anyone. Maybe they would remember a couple of noncops if she slowed and did something to draw their attention.

"If it's busy on the first floor, stay cool." He took hold of her forearm and squeezed hard.

Kate glanced up when the light ring came on around the number *1* and the elevator bell dinged. Mick had called the back entrance a good way to slip into the station unnoticed. Now Byer planned to slip her out?

There wouldn't be much time if she got away. Could she get to Cody before he did? Could she risk it?

They stepped into the narrow hallway and he steered her to the door. "Keep your head down."

Kate dropped back and released the sunglasses from her hand.

They clattered onto the floor.

"What the hell?"

"Sorry." She squatted down and retrieved the glasses, staring into the security camera for an instant before Byer pulled her to her feet and pushed her out the door into the afternoon heat.

"It pays to think like a cop, Kate. Lunch. Afternoon briefing while it settles. Perfect timing."

She wanted to resist but she let him pull her into the bustle of people moving down the street. They crossed and she expected he'd stop at a car parked next to the curb. That would be her chance, but he didn't stop.

Byer pulled her into a narrow alley and up a flight of metal stairs. The door at the top of the landing was solid and he slid a key into it. "Welcome to the nest, little bird." He opened the door, shoved her inside and twisted the dead bolt.

Kate kept her footing and watched him slide the chain guard into place.

She almost gagged on the air in the room. Everything from the sofa against one wall to the large brass bed in the corner was permeated with cigar smoke. The only window in the cubicle faced the police station across the street. Ornate black iron bars covered the opening on the outside and a filmy curtain rippled in the air currents sent out by an oscillating fan on the bedside table.

"Home."

"If you can call it that."

"What, you don't like it? I know it doesn't look like much, but it serves my purpose." He moved to the window and slid the curtain aside. "I want to see his face when he comes screaming out of there after he finds you gone. He'll assume I've taken you to the bayou, and I will when the time comes, but for now I want to watch. I might even let you have a look."

She sat down in one of the chairs next to a small square table and sized up the situation. She'd never be able to get the door open before he whipped out his knife. The walls of the building were brick, the window was barred. "Do you have a bathroom?"

"Next to the closet." He raised a spotting scope to his eye.

Standing up, she moved toward the narrow door. She turned the knob and pushed the door open. There was a toilet, sink and a shower stall, but no window. She stepped inside and shut the door. Her image in the medicine-cupboard mirror was drawn, ashen. Pulling off her cap, she shook out her hair and considered her options. Her cell phone was lying on Mick's desk, charging. Only the Taser was going to offer her the chance to get away, but what about his threat against Cody? Could she beat him to her child?

"Kate, get the hell out here," Byer shouted.

Panic flamed inside of her as she looked around the room in a desperate search for help. Her gaze settled on the bottle of soap next to the sink. "Just a minute." It wasn't much, but it might help.

She opened the door and came out of the bathroom.

"There's our boy." He motioned her over, grabbed her by the nape of the neck and forced her to look out of the second-story window.

Mick ran across the open sidewalk in front of the police station and climbed the steps. If she could just get his attention.

She lunged at the window and banged her hands against it. Maybe she could break it. Shattering glass falling on the sidewalk below would attract him, but the window didn't break, it was like hammering steel.

"Bulletproof glass." Byer laughed and released her neck, letting his arms encircle her waist. He pulled her against him. "Isn't this cozy? Him out there, us in here...alone at last."

Panic clawed her mind and she staved off nausea. This couldn't be happening.

Kate twisted against him and stumbled back.

The smolder of lust in his dark eyes quickly turned to rage. "Teasing little bitch." He balled his fist and stalked toward her. "Want to be with a real man? I can show you how it's done."

She looked at the door, then back at Byer, ready to defend herself until the last breath left her body, but he stopped abruptly and moved back to the window. What sort of mental trip was he on?

"Next time Kate, I'll…"

She turned away. Reprieve, but for how long?

"He's figuring it out right now. I hope his guts are exploding."

The rate of Byer's breathing accelerated. Rivers of sweat streaked the back of his neck. He was getting off thinking about Mick's reaction?

Byer's reality hit her like a hurricane. This was about Mick. It had never been about Natalie or herself.

Bret was fixated on Mick.

Panic crawled over her skin and she rubbed it away. Byer had followed Mick around since high school. College, the police force. His wife.

Her blood chilled in her skin. Live bait. She had to get away. Now.

Byer still held the spotting scope to his eye. If she could warn Mick, there'd still be time to get to Cody before Byer did.

Edging toward the door, she stilled the apprehension racing up and down her spine. She grasped the chain lock, careful to hold the links as she slid it open.

"Any minute now, he'll run out the door and look into the street, hoping to see you."

The link reached the end of the slide; she popped it out of the groove and pressed the chain against the doorjamb so it wouldn't rattle.

"You've got to see this, Kate. Here he comes, Mr. Great Cop."

She turned the dead bolt, every grind of the lock mechanism magnified in her ears. Too late, she heard the stomp of his approach.

A sound like the clap of thunder echoed in her eardrums and pain burned along the side of her head. She reeled, blinked back tears and grabbed the doorknob.

"Ah, Kate. You never disappoint." His breath was ragged, hot against her ear. "But I can't let you go." He cupped her nose and mouth with a rag.

The pungent smell of ether pushed into her lungs and she fought to breathe. Her mind raced to find a reason for the blackness that engulfed her. She closed her eyes, digging at his hand, while hopelessness coursed into her body.

"Go to sleep. When you wake up, I'll have something for you."

Her knees sagged. *No.* She tried to scream, but the word wouldn't leave her mind. *No.*

MICK COULDN'T STOP shaking as he scanned the faces of the people moving along the sidewalk. He'd guessed something was wrong when he'd reached his office and not found Kate there.

The computer was still on and when he'd moved the mouse, Cody's picture had popped onto the monitor screen. Maybe she'd decided to skip out and see him. He raked his fingers through his hair. She knew how dangerous it would be to go to him. Didn't she?

Maybe she'd headed over to Café du Monde without him? His gut twisted. Where was she? He stalked back into the station.

Murphy, the day clerk, was sitting behind the desk sipping a soda.

"Hey, Murf. You see a woman leave in the last hour? She'd be wearing a ball cap and sunglasses?"

"Um, I've been up to my butt in paperwork. Would that be your good-looking material witness?"

"Yeah."

"I'd have remembered her. I didn't see anyone."

Where was she? Mick's heart zinged into

overdrive. "Thanks. I'll check the recording room." He bolted for the security-tape booth. His emotions cranked up. Kate knew the dangers of going out alone. Maybe she'd been able to pull another vanishing act, but this time he'd have a record.

He stepped into the ten-by-ten room and searched the decks of video recorders until he found the back entrance. Stopping the tape, he hit eject and popped the video into the playback machine.

Frame by frame, he watched the tape until he saw something that rocked his soul. He advanced the image.

For an instant Kate looked up into the camera then dropped her head again. Byer's face flashed across the recording as he grabbed Kate and pushed her outside.

"Kate!" Mick's head spun as he raced for Schneider's office and threw open the door. "He's got her, Ben!"

"Who's got who?"

"Byer has Kate." Mick took several deep breaths; he couldn't think, couldn't clear his head. "I'm going to get her."

"We just came from his place. He's not holding her there."

Mick laid his face in his hands, working his

emotions. "He's sick. Probably always has been. Why didn't I see it?"

"You got a crystal ball shoved up your sleeve? You're no good to her like this. Keep thinking."

"Let's get an APB out." Mick pulled it together on the surface, but his heart was smashed. "We'll assume he's armed and dangerous."

Schneider looked straight at him. "He's good, Mick, but you're better."

"I don't feel better right now."

"Then get after him. Think like him. Be him."

Mick stood up and left the office, determined. He'd find Byer all right and when he did there'd be hell to pay. He wanted to put his hands around his throat and squeeze until he couldn't breathe anymore, until every miserable thought left his polluted mind.

The image of Kate stopping him tumbled through his thoughts and dropped him back into reality. He needed her. Cody needed her. A twist of emotion stretched deep inside of him awakening his awareness. He stepped into the elevator and hit the button.

He loved Kate Robear and no murdering son of a bitch was going to take her away.

Ever.

Chapter Sixteen

Mick sat back in his chair, bolted forward and stood up. His nerves were raw. He glanced at the clock on his office wall. Five-thirty and the APB hadn't produced Byer.

Cody's smiling face looked back at him from the computer screen. It was the last image Kate had seen and he couldn't close it.

Byer must have threatened Cody to get her out of the station. He was bold. Under the noses of a hundred cops, he'd walked in and taken her. Mick rubbed his eyes and rolled his head back and forth, trying to loosen the tension that had him in knots.

New Orleans was a big place; he could have taken her anywhere.

Frustration hissed through him; he paused at the window for the tenth time in as many minutes. Byer must have known when he left, must have seen him and timed his move perfectly. He'd have to be watching the front entrance.

Mick surveyed the row of old buildings across the street. Brick, most of them. Laced with ornate ironwork, period specific. Shops filled the street level, the balconies above spilled over with potted ferns and flowers in bloom in the afternoon heat.

He studied each structure. The overhead apartments were open. They wouldn't offer much in the way of concealment. The row was broken by an alley.

The hairs stood on the back of his neck. The next building was plain, no vegetated balcony, just a flat facade. A doughnut shop occupied the lower floor. The upper window above an awning was barred and the glass was covered with reflective film.

He holstered his gun and pulled on his jacket. It would go along with Byer's MO to be across the street, walking around above the heads of the cops eating doughnuts and conversing below. He was bold, with an ego to match.

Mick ran downstairs and poked his head into Schneider's office. "I'm going over to Betty's Place to check something out. Wanna come?"

"I try to stay away from that end of the block."

"No problem."

"Hey, Mick?"

"Yeah."

"I'm sorry Kate's life is in jeopardy. I get the impression…"

"She's more than a witness."

"Just keep it straight. You're a good cop. I'd hate to jerk your badge."

Were his emotions that transparent? "How soon will the feds be here?"

"Anytime. I'll brief them, see what they want to do, but Byer is ours."

"He's mine." Mick hit the front door and took the steps two at a time. Adrenaline surged inside him as he crossed the street and moved into the crowd. He imagined Bret forcing Kate down the sidewalk. He could feel her fear, taste the scream she must have held in, knowing he would kill Cody if she dared to let it out.

He paused, flattened himself against the wall and skirted the alleyway. He tried to look nonchalant, but his nerves were shot as he peered down the narrow corridor.

A flight of metal stairs were anchored to the brick wall. At the top there was a door. Mick scanned the length of the narrow passage, just wide enough for a car. It emptied onto the next street over.

He crossed to the doughnut shop and went inside. A couple of uniformed officers gabbed at a table in the corner. Patrons dotted the floor space, sitting at tables for two. The smell of coffee and fresh deep-fried doughnuts hung in the air. The smells usually woke up his taste buds, but not today.

A woman was behind the counter, sliding a tray of fresh glazed into the display case. She looked up. "What can I get you?"

"Information."

"Would you like that boxed?"

"Are you the owner?"

"Last time I checked."

"Do you have a renter upstairs?"

"Yeah."

"Has he got a name?"

"Are you a cop?" Her voice raised an octave.

He pulled his badge. "Jacoby, New Orleans P.D."

"Okay. That works. Never gave me his name. He came in here a couple of months ago, wanted to rent the loft. He flashed some cash and I took it. He's quiet. I haven't seen him since he moved in." She paused, then said, "But I did hear some commotion up there this afternoon. I don't know what he was doing."

"Tall? Dark hair?" Mick's guts tied in knots.

"Yeah."

"You got a key to the side door?"

"No. He installed a dead bolt, but for the kind

of money he gave me for the room, he can do whatever he wants."

Mick's thoughts cruised at a hundred miles an hour. Kate could be up there right now. He turned and walked to the uniforms' table. "Officer Jacoby. I need you both as backup. We've got a possible kidnap victim upstairs."

They both stood up, their coffee and half-eaten doughnuts forgotten.

"There's an APB out on this guy. He's armed and dangerous."

Mick led the way out the front door and they slipped around the corner into the alley. Mick dialed Schneider. "I think I found him. Across the street in the room above Betty's Place. Hurry."

The pull of restraint yanked on him, but he couldn't wait. He looked up the stairs at the door and unholstered his weapon. "Let's go." His feet on the metal steps made very little noise, but the officers behind him sounded like elephants. There'd be no element of surprise.

Mick reached the door just as Schneider rounded the corner. He stopped in the alley below, pulled his gun and nodded to Mick.

Mick rapped the door with his fist. "Byer. New Orleans Police. Open the door." No response. "We're coming in." Mick tried the handle, it turned in his hand. In surreal time, he stepped through the door and searched the dimly lit room over his pistol sight. It was empty. His heart dropped through his stomach.

"All clear." He turned to the two officers on the landing. "You can go back to Betty's. Schneider will assist."

They put their guns away and pounded down the stairs.

Schneider was joined by a couple of other detectives and they came up the stairway. "I've got CSI on the way. If there's forensic evidence in here, we'll get it."

He stepped back into the room. It was definitely Byer's holdup. It reeked of cigar smoke and covered any hint of Kate's light floral perfume. But he smelled her in his mind, remembered her fragrance as if he held her now. His throat tightened as memories of last night surfaced.

Schneider stepped into the room and left the other detectives outside on the landing. "We've got to protect this scene, Mick."

His gaze settled on a patch of blood, dark crimson against the white pillowcase. He moved in for a closer look, his heart pounding in his ears.

Strands of long dark hair were matted in the dried blood. Kate's hair. Kate's beautiful hair. Rage roared through him. "It's her blood, Ben.

That's her hair." He closed his eyes to beat back the horrific images that clouded his mind and threatened to consume him.

"We don't know that, not until forensics can take it to the lab."

"No damn lab has to confirm it for me."

"There's not enough there to prove anything. Pull yourself together or you're out of here."

Mick digested Schneider's words. He'd been at enough crime scenes to know what he meant. The volume of blood on the pillow wasn't fatal, but the hair mixed in with it indicated a head wound.

He took a deep breath and avoided the sight of the rumpled sheets. He couldn't let the thoughts that went along with that image hammer his mind into submission.

Stepping to the window, he looked outside. The curtain lay on the floor, still on the rod. Mick studied the glass, pulled a pen out of his pocket and tapped it. "Bulletproof. Tinted." He saw the spotting scope sitting on the sill. "He's been watching for a while. At least two months according to the landlady downstairs." Mick looked closer at the window surface. A smudge of fingerprints were on the glass.

"Look at this. A couple of prints."

"Good ones. We'll make sure they get lifted."

Turning away from the window, he avoided

the surface of the bed. He couldn't live with the thought of what might have happened on it. He'd kill Byer if he'd touched her.

"You better take off, Mick. Let me work this. You're too close. Get your head straight and come in tomorrow."

He looked into the bathroom. Tomorrow? Hell, he couldn't even believe there would be a tomorrow without her. His reflection stared back at him; he stepped closer and caught a glimpse of something on the medicine-cabinet mirror. He flicked on the light with his knuckle.

The letters *BG* were traced on the glass. They were formed by some sort of clear liquid. Mick looked down at the bottle of soft soap next to the sink. "That's my girl." The air caught in his throat. She was always thinking, always challenging him to think harder.

"What'd you say, Jacoby?"

"*BG*. That's where he's taken her." Chilled calm took shape inside of him. His gut told him she was still alive. Byer wanted him to witness her pain firsthand, in person.

"So what are we waiting for, an invitation?"

As long as he held back and stayed away, she'd continue to live. It was a desperate game he planned to play.

"He expects me to charge in and leave my

brain in the car. The minute I get close enough to take him, he'll kill her."

"If that's your spin on things, I want you to talk to Dr. Rand in psychology. They can put a profile together on this sick bastard."

"I don't need a shrink to lay it out. Byer is my shadow, my nemesis. Has been since high school. The scary part is, I encouraged him. His home life was hell on earth, an abusive mother, nonexistent father. He showed up in an at-risk youth program my dad spearheaded. We tried to help. Pushed him mentally and physically in academics and sports. Natalie came along while we were at LSU. She was hot on Bret. He fell for her, but I liked her, too. The competition got brutal…I just never guessed how obsessed he was."

Mick shook his head. The air in the room felt heavy, along with his heart. "I loved her, Ben." He looked into his friend's eyes and saw sympathy. "But that love signed their death warrants."

"Don't do this, buddy. Strolling down memory lane with a wacko like Byer will make you crazy."

"It's okay. I've made my peace with the past—I'm moving on now, it's Kate I have to save. She's innocent. Tossed into this sick scenario by Byer. I'd bet my life he stole the 944 from her, knowing it would be easy to sacrifice a Robear. Who'd believe a car thief had their car stolen? Poetic justice."

"That's great. I'm glad you have it all figured out, but mental crime solving has to be backed up by evidence. I've got Special Agent Monroe over in my office. He wants you to wear a wire."

"I can try to get him to confess to money laundering, but I'm there for Kate."

"Enough said. We'll give him his inside sound bite. He'll have to hope Byer says something he can use."

"I think I know where he is."

"Maybe you'd like to share." Ben glared at him.

"Otis Whittley's place. He doesn't think I'm smart enough to find him, so he'll pick a place I know, just to make sure I show up. He's after gratification. Nothing else matters."

Excitement and worry churned his insides. Was he calling Byer right? Had he decoded his screwed-up logic until it made sense in a crazy sort of way?

"She's still alive. I can feel it." It was really his heart he knew was tethered to hers. He wanted to whisper to her again in the darkness, in the heat of lovemaking, in the slow burn that followed their connection.

"I hope you're right, son."

Chapter Seventeen

Kate opened her eyes and closed them several times, squinting against the flat light coming through a curtainless window. The effort sent a sensation equivalent to tiny jackhammers pounding into her head. What time was it? Where was she?

Focusing her vision on the soiled mattress she lay on, she attempted to pull her left arm out from behind her back so she could read her watch, but it wouldn't move.

Reality drummed in her brain. Her hands were tied, the rope biting into her flesh with every attempt to move.

One by one she put the events together through a haze that blanketed her mind. She'd been dragged into the room, her ankles and hands tied. She could feel the pressure of duct tape on her mouth, smell the chemical odor of adhesive.

Struggling to the edge of the bed, she swung her legs off and pushed herself into an upright position. The taste of blood in her mouth turned her stomach. She swallowed and scanned the room. It was somehow familiar. Byer had said he was taking her to Bayou Gauche. Otis Whittley. He'd brought her to Otis's shack?

She surveyed the room in the fading light and saw a miracle. Her heart jumped into her throat. Her backpack lay in the corner behind the closed door. If she could get her backpack, she could access her knife, cut her hands loose....

Slowly, she stood up, but the room began to spin and she rocked like a toy horse. She sat back down, fought for balance and staved off a wave of nausea. A string of memories cut through the cloud in her mind. Ether.

A couple of deep breaths helped to clear her head. Physically she was intact, but she'd have to crawl to her backpack or risk having Byer hear her fall and come into the room.

Kate slid off the bed and balanced her weight until she touched down on the floor. She lay down on her side. With her feet she pushed against the floor and slid, inch by inch, toward the corner.

Another round of nausea swept over her. She

let it pass and again bent her knees and extended them, every push bringing her closer to escape.

Halfway there, she caught sight of movement outside the window. Kate froze, watching as a face peered through the glass and into the room. Mick?

She blinked hard, praying it was really him and not a hallucination. She was glad the tape held his name in, but her mind screamed *caution*.

Byer was waiting for him. Did he have any idea how sick Byer was?

Pushing off again, she watched his shadow move away from the window. Panic drove her harder and beads of sweat formed on her forehead. He was walking into Byer's trap. She couldn't let it happen.

The tap of Byer's footsteps in the living room stopped.

She went still. Waiting. Listening. Any minute she expected the crack of gunfire. Closing her eyes she tried to focus, but the pounding of Byer's footsteps coming down the hall drove terror through her heart.

Was he coming for her?

Curling into a ball, she held the cry in her throat.

The footsteps stopped.

She opened her eyes and spotted the toes of Byer's boots through the crack at the bottom of the door. Did he know Mick was outside? She lay so still she could hear the sound of her heartbeat in her ears.

The door creaked open.

She held her breath.

Byer stalked into the room and stopped at the bed. "Where are you!" he yelled.

The splintering of wood pulled his head around and he bolted out of the room.

"You son of a bitch," Mick roared. "Where is she?"

His entrance drove her forward. She shuffled to her backpack as all hell broke loose in the living room. Grunts of mortal combat cemented her determination. She wasn't going to lose the man she loved to his rage or a madman.

With her hands tied she slid the zipper.

A shot went off in the living room.

She froze; dread danced inside of her. *Come on. Come on.* She put her hands into her backpack, fishing until she found her Swiss Army knife. In four slices she cut through the rope. She sat up, clarity replacing cloudiness.

Another shot went off.

Kate sawed through the rope binding her ankles and pulled the tape off her mouth.

Reaching into the backpack she pulled out her Taser, cupped it in her hand and crawled toward the open door. Poking her head out she tried to see down the hallway.

Reality invaded her mind and she felt herself being hauled up from the floor. She'd neglected to check behind her.

Kate looked down at Byer's boots. Felt his arm around her waist as he crushed her against him for a shield, but there was something next to his feet.

Red and spreading fast.

Blood.

"Here she is, Jacoby. What's left." His chest heaved against her back. Wetness soaked her shirt. It was coming from him. She positioned the Taser in her hand.

"She's not as good as Natalie. Natalie was fine. She was the only woman I ever loved and you took her." He pushed her into the living room.

Mick stood in the ready position, his focus locked on the gun muzzle against Kate's temple. His heart pounded in his ears.

"Let her go, Bret. I'm the one you want. Don't take it out on Kate."

"You've got a hell of a mouth, Jacoby. I always hated it when you were right, but I didn't get you out here to kill you first. I've got my favorite knife, saved it just for her."

Mick sized up the length of the leather sheath strapped onto Byer's right thigh. It was a hell of a knife. He swallowed. "Why'd you do it, Bret? Why'd you kill Natalie and Megan?"

"She didn't want me anymore." He paused for a minute, his face contorted by madness. "She threatened to tell you all about me. I couldn't let her do it. There wasn't any other way."

"What about Whittley and Romaro? Was that the only way you had to deal with them?"

"Double-crossing scum. Whittley put the screws to me with that car. Everyone wanted something that was mine." Byer's eyes went wide and wild as he fixed a stare on Mick.

"The only woman I loved was yours. Once again the jock, Mick, had it all, but I had her right under your nose. In your own damn bed."

Mick remembered the picture in Byer's trophy gallery. Natalie's inviting smile. The truth penetrated him like a dagger, but the pain was fleeting. Byer and Natalie were lovers, he had taken the picture as a trophy.

"What are you going to do with Kate?"

"Don't you get it? I picked her to bring you to me. I planted the Robear name on the street and watched it grow. I even used her car to level your family, and it worked, didn't it. Here you are, and she's about to die. I bested you. For payback, she goes first."

"No!" Kate ducked away from the gun muzzle, jammed the Taser against Byer's side and pressed the button.

The gun went off, piercing her eardrums and singeing her nostrils with the smell of gunpowder.

In slow motion she watched a bullet slam into Mick's chest and blow him backward.

Byer released her and collapsed on the floor.

"Mick!" Kate raced to his side. He was already trying to sit up. Her heart hammered in her chest. "You're hit."

"I wore my vest."

"I knew you'd come."

Mick leaned close to Byer and kicked his gun away. "Wouldn't have missed it, babe." He kissed her, then looked her over. "Ouch." Mick brushed the goose egg on the side of her head. "We better get that looked at."

The flash of a knife blade low and right grabbed his focus. Seconds clicked in his mind; Byer's intention was clear.

Kate...he had to save Kate.

Mick squeezed her against him and rolled hard to the left as Byer's knife blade sliced toward her.

Her scream of pain and surprise rattled his eardrums, but he'd put some distance between them.

"Hang on." He jumped to his feet and raised his gun. "Stop, Byer!"

"Go to hell," Byer bellowed and charged forward, the knife raised high, hatred burning in his eyes.

Mick squeezed the trigger in rapid succession. Bullets split the air in the room.

Byer's face contorted in pain, then a victorious smile spread over his lips. He hit the floor like a rock.

Kate's gasps pulled Mick back into real time.

He knelt next to her, assessing the volume of blood soaking the sleeve of her shirt from the slice of Byer's knife. "We got him, Kate. We got him." He pulled her into his arms, rocking her like a child.

Relief spread through his body as he spoke into the concealed microphone. "We need an ambulance out here. Kate's been injured."

She lay in Mick's arms letting his warmth and nearness calm her fears. The sight of Bret Byer sprawled next to them was unnerving, but he wasn't going to hurt them ever again. "We're a good team, Mick."

He kissed her forehead. "I'd say we're a winning team tonight."

"I'm glad it's over." She didn't want them to be over.

She watched him pull the top buttons open on his shirt and jerk out a thin wire with a round device on the end.

"Eavesdroppers. Byer's confession will clear you." He pulled the leads out of the microphone and tossed it across the room.

"I've been thinking… I don't know what I'd do without you, and I just came too close to finding out."

She looked into his face, saw the question in his eyes and knew the answer. "I had the same thought."

He kissed her again. In the distance she heard the wail of sirens.

"There's this little cottage I have the use of out in Slidell…."

"Can I come?"

"I've been taken for a ride by a Robear, but I didn't plan on having my heart dragged along."

"It's not so bad, is it?"

He lowered his mouth to hers, tasting the sweetness of her kiss, letting a surge of desire go unchecked. "No, but it looks like the hunt is over, and as impossible as it seems, I finally caught one."

She smiled up at him and he brushed her cheek

with his fingers. Love pulsed in his veins, a love he wanted to share with her. "I love you, Kate."

Her eyes took on a misty glow, a glitter of excitement.

"Can I sentence you to a life term with me?"

"Only if I'm guilty."

"Are you?" he asked.

She looked away, but he pulled her chin back toward him and searched her face.

"My only crime, Officer, is loving you. The statute of limitations has expired on everything else."

Epilogue

Mick scooped Cody into his arms as they made their way to the front entrance of the nursing home.

Kate managed a smile for both of the guys in her life, even though her stomach churned. They were there to see Jake. She was there to say goodbye. Dylan was going to take over responsibility for Jake's care.

She took Mick's hand, feeling a surge of gumption. He'd managed to convince her that Jake had taken her dare on his own. She was slowly beginning to believe it was true. Everyone was responsible for their decisions, good or bad, and the consequences of those decisions in the end.

"It's down here." She led Mick to the end of the hall and into a room. The blinds were drawn. Jake's wheelchair was in the corner.

"Jake, Cody's here to see you."

The hum of the automatic chair stopped her and she watched the chair turn.

Mick was next to her. He let go of her hand and put Cody down. "I'm going to get a coffee. Do you want anything?"

"No, thank you." She watched him leave, knowing he'd sensed her discomfort with the situation. He was giving her the space she needed. When she turned back around, Jake was looking at her. She saw his gaze drift to Mick's retreating back and then he looked back to her, a half grin on his face.

"Dylan told me…." he whispered. The respirator forced another whoosh of air into his lungs. "I want you to be happy." His voice faded with the exhale. "Go, Kate. Go to him."

Warm tears, grateful tears, stung her eyes. She touched his cheek and put Cody's hand onto his. "Thank you."

She fled the room, overwhelmed by the weight of Jake's forgiveness.

"Mick." She spotted him at the vending machine, dropping in some change. Racing to him, she put her arms around his neck.

He held her close as she sobbed against him. "It's going to work out, Kate." Mick soothed her, knowing the battle of emotions that raged inside of her. The line she'd connected between herself and Jake had evaporated. And with it, her reasons for being bound to him.

"He's receiving the best care possible. He'll continue to get good care. You can let go."

She stepped back from him and smiled. "I know."

"We'll get Cody out here every chance we get."

"Thank you."

He stroked her cheek, overcome with need. They'd been together every night since Byer died and he never wanted to spend a night without her.

"Want a cup?" He selected his choice and pushed the button.

"No thanks. My nerves are shot."

Mick fingered the engagement ring he'd slipped on her left hand. "They found a stack of cash at Whittley's place. He rat-holed it in the bathroom floor. After your testimony next week, you can walk out of the courtroom and never look back." She squeezed his hand and he worked to keep his desire under control.

"Thank God. It proves I didn't take it."

"What do you say we pack up and spend some time at the cottage? I've got some leave coming."

"I'd like that." She brushed her tears away and stared into his eyes. A mixture of happiness and relief spread through her, working its way into her soul.

Jake had given her his forgiveness; the justice system, immunity, but Mick had given her his heart, and there wasn't anything else she needed in this life.

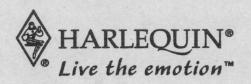
HARLEQUIN®
Live the emotion™

AMERICAN *Romance*®

Upbeat,
All-American Romances

flipside

Romantic Comedy

Harlequin Historicals®

Historical,
Romantic Adventure

HARLEQUIN®
INTRIGUE®

Romantic Suspense

HARLEQUIN®
HARLEQUIN ROMANCE®

The essence of
modern romance

HARLEQUIN®
Presents®

Seduction and passion
guaranteed

HARLEQUIN® *Super*ROMANCE®

Emotional,
Exciting, Unexpected

Temptation®

Sassy, Sexy, Seductive!

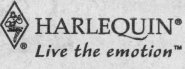

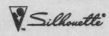